D1737277

Dragonfly in the Land of Ice

RESA NELSON

ISBN: **1518695949**
ISBN-13: **978-1518695940**

ACKNOWLEDGEMENTS

Many thanks to my fellow authors, Carla Johnson and Frank Stearns, who read this novel before publication and gave me excellent feedback.

Also by Resa Nelson

The Dragonslayer Series:

The Dragonslayer's Sword (Book 1)
The Iron Maiden (Book 2)
The Stone of Darkness (Book 3)
The Dragon's Egg (Book 4)

The Dragonfly Series:

Dragonfly (Book 1)

Standalone novels:

Our Lady of the Absolute
All of Us Were Sophie

CHAPTER 1

"I'm not mortal," Greeta said, facing her family. "Am I?"

Instead of answering, neither Papa nor Auntie Peppa could meet her gaze or offer an immediate answer.

Greeta took a deep breath, angry and disappointed with the people she loved the most. "I imagine we have a long journey ahead of us and plenty of time for you to tell me the truth about who I really am."

Not terribly long ago, Greeta had stood on the beach, startled by the sight of a Northlander ship on the ocean's horizon. Today she found herself on that very ship, its smooth wooden boards pitching beneath her feet and forcing her to cling to a side rail for balance. Seawater sprayed across her face, leaving salt on her lips.

The crew of a dozen tall and blond Northlander men raced along the ship's sleek and narrow length, shouting to each other and laughing. Their pale faces were sunburned from what must have been several days at sea. Unlike the people of the home Greeta had always known, a village of the Shining Star nation, these Northlanders wore brightly colored linen pants and shirts. Silver rings crowded their fingers. A few men wore armbands of silver as well.

"Poor little dragon girl," said the man with the broken nose, his tone mocking and cruel. He stood before Greeta and her family, arms crossed and stern-faced.

The man with a lumpy forehead smacked his colleague in the arm. "Ain't no way to speak to our pretty little guest."

"Guest!" Appalled, Greeta turned her attention from her family to the men who had kidnapped her moments ago. "Who do you think you are to call me your guest?"

Grinning, the lumpy man said, "I be Thorkel, and the grumpy one here be Rognvald."

"Grumpy?" Rognvald rolled his eyes.

"Just because I'm practical, not dreamy-eyed like the likes of you."

Not knowing what to make of the North-landers in command of the ship, Greeta said, "Who are you people?"

Thorkel brightened. "Friends of your mother."

Rognvald snorted. "Weren't no friend of mine. Enemies more like it."

Whispering, Thorkel pointed at Rognvald. "He pretends he don't want no friends. But your mum be a good friend to us both." His expression fell into sadness. "Especially when things got rough."

Greeta considered her family's silence and decided her chances of getting answers were better with these strangers who had hauled her onboard just minutes ago. "Why did you call me a dragon girl?"

Now Papa jumped to his feet. "Thorkel, no!"

Greeta couldn't tell if Thorkel didn't hear Papa or chose to ignore him. Answering Greeta's question, Thorkel said, "Because that's how you be when we first met."

She eyed him with suspicion. "What exactly do you mean?"

Thorkel spoke plainly and clearly, as if that would help explain his meaning. "A. Dragon. Girl."

Rognvald said, "Not a dragon girl. A dragon. Just hatched from the shell by the size of it."

"A dragon?" The pitch beneath Greeta's feet became violent, and she struggled to maintain her balance. Her head swam with the information. Not long ago she'd turned into a dragon, but she still didn't understand how or why it happened. For all she knew, it might have been something she ate that made her shapeshift. But now these men were saying she'd been *born* in dragon shape, not mortal!

"Just as I said!" Thorkel straightened out one arm and gestured a spiral around it with his other hand. "Used to wrap yourself around your father's arm. Such a sweet thing."

Greeta remembered the day she'd first seen this ship on the horizon. For a moment, she'd had a faint recollection of curling around Papa's arm when she was a baby.

I wasn't remembering something that happened when I was a baby. I remember-

ed being a hatchling dragon!

Rognvald shook his head. "Wouldn't have been so sweet if she'd bit us and killed us." He eyed her, keeping a careful distance. "Ain't so sure her bite wouldn't kill us right now."

Thorkel slapped his comrade heartily on the back. "Even better! Think of the good she can do us back home." Responding to Rognvald's quizzical expression, Thorkel added, "She can bite those we need her to bite. Not us."

The ship's large square sail snapped in the wind. The vessel's low rails made it feel like a sea creature skimming just above the water's surface. Still dressed in a man's shirt and breeches, which she had borrowed after returning to her human form a few days ago, Greeta felt them grow damp from the constant sea spray. She touched the dragonfly pendant she wore on a leather thong around her neck. The one she'd lost and Red Feather had returned to her. Thinking about Red Feather now brought a lump to her throat. But this wasn't the time to miss him. That would have to wait. Facing her family, she said, "Why didn't you tell me?"

Papa looked up at her with sorrowful eyes. "You turned mortal soon as we got here. Always were mortal since then."

Auntie Peppa put a supporting arm around Papa's shoulders. "We thought you were done being a dragon. There was no reason to think it would ever happen again."

When the ship pitched again, its strength came close to making Greeta topple over. But she found her balance and stood tall. "But I did turn into a dragon. I don't know how or why it happened. And I don't know why I became mortal again. But Red Feather and his brothers told me I'm a shapechanger. Is that what I am?"

Before Papa or Auntie Peppa could answer, Thorkel laughed and said, "Of course! Your mum was a shapeshifter. Why wouldn't you be one, too?"

CHAPTER 2

"Thorkel, enough!" Papa said, his voice low and angry. "It's our business, not yours."

Rognvald nudged Thorkel. "Ain't right to meddle much. Leave them be." Rognvald walked away with a reluctant Thorkel following.

Heaving a weary sigh, Papa said, "Any Northlander who ate dragon meat could change shape. Your mother grew up in Guell. That village had its own dragonslayer and a steady supply of dragon meat."

Everything Papa said made Greeta queasy. "I don't understand. People turned into dragons and ate each other?"

"No!" Auntie Peppa said. "It wasn't like

that at all."

"I ate dragon meat myself and changed shape," Papa said.

"Papa, no!" Greeta wrapped her arms around herself. "I was a dragon! Maybe I still am."

Auntie Peppa waved her hands as if washing away words hanging in the air. "We're not telling it right. The first thing you need to understand is that there are two different types of dragons. Do you remember the stories your Uncle Killing Crow has told you about bears?"

Greeta nodded, although still shaken from the idea that her own father had eaten dragon meat. "Of course. Even though all animals are our brothers and sisters, some bears don't respond to the respect we give them."

"Yes," Auntie Peppa said. "And if you encounter such a bear, you must do whatever is necessary to protect yourself."

"Even if that means killing it," Greeta said. "So one kind of dragon is like an angry bear that could kill you if you don't kill it first?"

"That's right," Papa said. "That's what dragonslayers killed and what people ate."

Greeta paused, imagining such a thing. But after having the experience of actually being a dragon just a few days ago pushed her back to the brink of feeling sick again. "So if they ate dragon meat they turned into dragons?"

"No," Auntie Peppa said. "All anyone could do was shift their shape a little bit. Change the color of their hair or become prettier or grow taller."

Papa cleared his throat. "Your mama changed her shape to do her blacksmithing. She figured she needed the strength of a man, so she made herself taller and made her muscles bigger. Mostly people let her be when she worked because they knew she felt embarrassed at the way she made herself look."

Greeta remembered how she'd walked in the Dreamtime during the past few weeks and the ghost women she'd met there, including the one who claimed to be her mother. "What did she look like?"

"We told you all your life," Auntie Peppa said too quickly. "She looked like us, of course."

"Enough," Papa said, his voice soft now. "Your mama had a rough start to life. She once looked like any Northlander but when she was just a little thing she ended up covered with scars. Her family did it. Locked her in a cage with a dragon that chewed her up. Those people did it for their own benefit. Having to do with magic."

Auntie Peppa's face twisted with worry. "Careful, Trep."

Papa gave an acknowledging nod to Auntie Peppa and continued. "So when your mother got away she made herself look different because she didn't want to be like them." Papa laughed. "She made herself the opposite of them: short, dark haired, dark eyed, dark skinned. Much like the Shining Star people, even though she didn't know such people existed."

Auntie Peppa spoke up again. "Trep, please."

He put a gentle hand on his sister's shoulder. "No need to shield the girl anymore."

Fascinated by his response, Greeta jumped in to learn more. "Shield me from what?"

Papa met her gaze directly and spoke to her with the same respect he gave to Auntie Peppa. "The last time I saw your mama we was planning to make a life together. But then she disappeared. I don't know what happened to her, but we think she must have turned into a dragon because I found an egg." He hesitated. "Didn't find it. Was given to me."

Auntie Peppa fidgeted. "Trep, you told me you promised her not to tell anyone."

"She said I could tell family. And Greeta's family."

"My mother?" Greeta said. "She told you that?"

Papa shook his head. "No. Was one of the gods that told me."

CHAPTER 3

Before Papa could say more, Thorkel interrupted them. "Looks like rough seas ahead. Could use some more hands to help." He nodded at Greeta. "Good time for her to learn how to pitch in."

For the remainder of the day Greeta learned how to raise and lower the sail, steer the ship, and tie knots. All the time, she kept looking back from where they'd come, even long after the shore had disappeared from sight. She worried about everyone and everything she'd left behind.

After the sun had set and everyone settled below deck for the night, she tried to raise the subject of Papa's past encounter with a god and what the god had told Papa he could never discuss with anyone but family.

"Now's not the time," Papa whispered. "Not until we can speak alone."

"You've already said too much," Auntie Peppa said. She nestled in a corner and wrapped a blanket around her shoulders. "It's put us at too much risk."

Weary from the day, Greeta spoke her mind. "I want to go home. I want to be with our people. The Shining Star people." She glared at the beefy men spread out on the floor of the lower deck while they snored. "Not these savages."

"They ain't savages," Papa said with a sharpness to his tone that Greeta rarely heard. "They're Northlanders. Just like us."

"You don't understand." Greeta whispered, not wanting to wake any of the Northlander men. "When Shadow took me away to learn how to walk in the Dreamtime, something separated me from her. I was lost. And then some men took me captive and gave me to a Northlander man."

Auntie Peppa said, "We're the only Northlanders in the Great Turtle Lands."

"No," Greeta said. "There's another. But I think he might be dangerous." Turning to her father, she said, "You sent Red Feather and his brothers to find me, and they succeeded. But the Northlander's men tried to kill them. And yet Red Feather and his brothers lived and helped me get free. The Northlander man vanished, but he might be a threat to our people. I have to warn them."

"We made a promise to help Thorkel and Rognvald," Papa said. "They helped us years ago. It's our time to help them."

"No!" Greeta said, astonished by her father's stubbornness. "Our people come first!"

"How does this Northlander man you met plan to hurt the Shining Star people?" Auntie Peppa said.

"I don't know. Not for certain." Greeta hesitated. "But from everything I heard him say, I suspect he wants to bring them under his control."

Papa and Auntie Peppa laughed.

"How can you make light of this?" Greeta said, feeling more worried and desperate by the moment. "Everyone is in terrible danger!"

Auntie Peppa winked at her. "You mean the brave and strong men in our village? The ones who hunt bears and bison? The ones who know days before anyone comes to our village because they sense their presence in the wind?"

Greeta took Auntie Peppa's point. The Shining Star men in their village had prevented raids and attacks for as long as Greeta could remember, because they'd travel to meet trouble before it arrived on their doorstep. They had a remarkable knack for detecting outsiders and making peace with them that Greeta had never understood. "But what if the Northlander man I met is craftier than the men in our village?"

Papa and Auntie Peppa laughed again. "No need to fret none about that," Papa said. "When you known anybody to be smarter than them?"

Greeta had no answer.

"Go to sleep," Auntie Peppa said. "And trouble yourself no more with any worries."

Greeta listened to Papa and Auntie Peppa fall asleep, their breath becoming slow and deep. Perhaps they were right. Even so, Greeta couldn't stop thinking about the home from which she'd been taken.

During the past many days she'd been ridiculed by strangers, taken captive, and turned into a dragon. Now all Greeta wanted was to go back to her normal, everyday life. She longed to wake in the morning and take a casual stroll along the shore to look for food. She wanted to spend time with her family and friends. She felt happiest when her days were simple and carefree.

I don't like being stolen away without my permission. I don't like being told I have to help strangers when it's my own people who likely need my help. I don't like being dragged to strange places by strange people.

I want my life back. I want to go home.

Before Greeta drifted to sleep, she remembered that her family had told her that two types of dragons existed and the first type acted like bears that killed people instead of respecting them.

For a brief moment, she realized Papa hadn't explained the other type of dragon.

* * *

The journey across the great ocean lasted several days. Greeta agreed to help the Northlanders in whatever way her family wished, but she saw this time as something brief and temporary. Soon she expected to be traveling back to her home in the Shining Star village.

She cared about her own world, not that of the Northlanders.

On the sixth morning of the voyage, land finally came into sight.

Greeta helped the crew lower the sail and put it away. She followed their lead in taking an oar from the stack in the center of the ship. Finding an empty spot at the back of the ship, she notched her oar in place and matched the rhythm of the men rowing behind her. She marveled at the way the ship responded, now racing through the shallow waters toward the shore. Minutes later, the ship slid up to a simple wooden dock on the beach.

Stepping toward the masthead carved in the shape of a dragon's fearsome head, Greeta sat on the low rail and swung her feet over it.

Some distance away, a young woman waved her arms over her head. "Go away!" she shouted. "You're not welcome here!"

She then marched away in disgust.

Thorkel stood on the dock. "Never mind her. It's only my daughter. We have a bit of a disagreement, but don't bother to trouble yourself none over it." Beaming, he offered a hand to Greeta, helping her take the short jump from the rail to the dock. "Welcome to our home," he said. "Welcome to the Land of Ice. Just over there's our house in the settlement we made some twenty years ago. We call the place Blackstone."

Greeta stood in awe of the land before her, beginning with a beach made of pitch-black sand that sparkled in direct sunlight. Bright green grassy fields stretched beyond the beach. The houses in Blackstone were made of stone walls and sod roofs thick with grass. Thin pillars of smoke escaped from the center of each roof. Men and women strolled in and out of the homes while small children ran in circles chasing cackling chickens. Like Thorkel, Rognvald, and their crew, the men wore trousers and shirts dyed in bright colors: yellows, blues, reds, and greens. The women wore long dresses in the same bright colors. To the right of the fields, a towering cliff faced the sea, rumbling with a high and powerful waterfall.

And in the far distance she saw a mountain made of ice, sparkling and gleaming in the sunlight.

Turning to Thorkel, she said, "I thought the whole land would be made of ice."

"We be grateful for what ice there is." Pointing at the waterfall, Thorkel said, "Gives us the best water you ever tasted." Turning back to the ship, he gave a hand to help Auntie Peppa step onto the dock, followed by Papa.

Neither of them looked at the land with the same wonder that Greeta felt. But then she remembered they'd been here before continuing to the Great Turtle Lands.

"You promised to say why you need our help once we got here," Papa said. "Let's get to it so we can be done and on our way back home."

Shouldering a bag of supplies from the ship, Rognvald joined them. "It's about that mountain." His face twisted with a look of disgust. "And the ice dragons that come from it."

Auntie Peppa paled. "Ice dragons?"

Papa crossed his arms, cocking his

head to one side with the expression he always had when he thought someone meant to fool him. "Is that what you call dragons that live on a mountain made of ice? Or are you saying the dragons themselves are made of ice?"

Thorkel waved his hands as if brushing away the questions. "Plenty of time to explain later. It be time for supper, and I smell my wife's good cooking from here. Come eat with us."

Greeta turned her attention to the air. Until now she'd only noticed the sharp scent of the sea. She paid close attention when the wind shifted, delighted at the hearty tang of spiced broth.

Leaving the crew behind to secure the ship and unload it, Greeta and her family followed Thorkel and Rognvald, who argued with him at every step. "Ain't no sense in waiting for another attack," Rognvald said. "We've too much to lose. Especially with winter creeping around the corner."

Greeta nudged her father and whispered, "Winter?"

"We're far up in the north," Papa said. "Winter comes sooner and lasts half the year. Their summer begins and ends in the blink of an eye."

The Land of Ice. That's why they call it that.

Auntie Peppa leaned in and whispered, "I'm not worried about the winter so much as the attacks. What have we gotten ourselves into?"

"Keeping our word," Papa said, his jaw set in grim determination. "They helped us years ago, and now we promised to help them in return. We keep our promises."

Entering the settlement of small stone homes, Greeta noticed a group of young men and women carrying pails of water into the village, walking a path that led to the nearby waterfall. All stood tall and beautiful, long blonde hair falling to the waists of men and women alike. The sight of them made her nervous.

Why do I feel this way? It doesn't make any sense. They're like me. Just like me. Not like back home.

Greeta's breath caught in her throat. That was it. She had lived all her life being the different one, taller and paler than anyone her age. For the first time in her life, she found herself looking at peers.

Real peers who looked just like her.

So why do I feel so afraid of them?

Greeta noticed one man whose laughter and confident walk reminded her of why she had once loved Wapiti, the man who had been her sweetheart since childhood in the Shining Star village back home. Wapiti had proven himself to be weak-minded and disloyal. Although Greeta longed for the love she had once had with him, she knew that love had died.

Oddly enough, she found herself thinking about Wapiti's brother Red Feather.

Why am I thinking about him again?

Greeta didn't want to admit it to herself, but she knew the answer. When she needed help, Wapiti did nothing. Red Feather had been the one who stood by Greeta's side, no matter what.

She shook her head to clear it.

The young Northlander man looked up from the group surrounding him and stared at Greeta as if he had read her mind.

Even from this distance, Greeta felt his gaze lock with hers and sensed a mutual sense of curiosity. Shyness overwhelmed her, and she felt like a small child wanting to hide behind Auntie Peppa's skirt. Greeta looked away, unable to look at the young Northlander any longer.

"Molly!" Thorkel shouted, racing toward the first stone home on the edge of Blackstone.

Greeta tried to figure out who Molly might be. His wife? His little girl? She saw no one near the home who responded to his call.

Instead, an animal unlike anything Greeta had ever seen bleated from where it grazed on the grass on top of the home's sod roof. Standing on black legs as thin as sticks, the creature looked as white and puffy as a cloud pulled out of the sky.

"Come here, Molly girl!" Thorkel shouted, throwing his arms open wide where he stood at the edge of the sod roof.

The cloud-like animal stepped to the roof's edge with tentative feet, looking from the edge to Thorkel's open arms and back to the edge again.

"You and that stupid sheep," Rognvald muttered, pacing behind Thorkel.

"Sheep?" Greeta turned to Papa and Auntie Peppa.

Auntie Peppa looked at Papa. "I forgot. They don't have sheep in the Great Turtle

Lands."

Rognvald shook his head in exaspera-
tion and walked away. To Thorkel he said,
"I leave you to your sheep. Got to see my
own family."

"A sheep is just a farm animal," Papa
told Greeta. "One that makes for good eating."

The sheep on top of Thorkel's roof bleated louder and backed away from the edge
as if changing its mind.

Thorkel turned, his face drawn in distress. "Hush!" he whispered. Turning back
toward his home, Thorkel raised his voice.
"Don't you pay them no mind, Molly. No
one be meaning you any harm. Come to
your papa."

Without warning, the animal leapt toward him. Thorkel caught the sheep in his
arms with the same ease as if someone
has tossed a potato into his hands. He
kissed the animal on top of its head.
"That's my girl, Molly!" Thorkel placed
Molly on the ground and swatted her
rump. "Now be along with you. Go play
with your mates."

A woman's voice called out from the
small stone house. "Molly! Honestly, Fa-

ther, you care more about that animal than you do about your own children!"

Greeta stared at the open door to the home, intrigued by the voice and wondering what Thorkel's children were like.

Until she remembered one had met the ship with anger just a short while ago. Although Thorkel's daughter had stood too far inland to be recognizable, Greeta knew her voice belonged to the one they'd already seen from a distance.

The young woman who emerged from the house stepped outside and paused, placing her hands on her hips while she studied Greeta, Papa, and Auntie Peppa. "So these are the people who can help us kill the ice dragons?" Disappointment strained her face. "How many times do I have to tell you that we need no help? Especially not from strangers. They'll only make things worse!"

Greeta stared at Thorkel's daughter in astonishment. She didn't look like any Northlander Greeta had ever seen. The daughter had Thorkel's height, but everything else about her appearance made the young woman look like a member of the Shining Star nation.

CHAPTER 4

Startled by the appearance of Thorkel's daughter, Greeta blurted, "Are you from the Great Turtle Lands? Were you born there?"

Thorkel's daughter wore an outfit made of layers. The outermost looked like a lightweight red coat gaping open in the front. Underneath, she wore a bright blue dress with a neckline straight below her collarbones. A light beige under-dress peeked above with an open neckline at her throat. At each shoulder a large silver brooch pinned the red over-dress to the blue dress, and a string of amber and silver beads connected the brooches. A dagger was tucked under the leather belt looped around her waist. She stood shoulder-to-shoulder with her father, but her long hair and eyes were as black as the sand on the beach. Instead of pale skin that turned pink in the sun, her skin was a light golden brown.

Thorkel's daughter stared at Greeta as if she'd shapeshifted into Molly the sheep. To her father, she said, "I thought you said they're Northlanders."

"Of course they be Northlanders," Thorkel said, gesturing at Greeta, Papa, and Auntie Peppa. "You can tell that by looking at them."

His daughter pointed at Greeta. "Then why does that one speak gibberish?"

"Gibberish?" Greeta repeated, confused by the accusation.

Thorkel's daughter waved her hands, reminding Greeta of Thorkel's tendency to do the same. Like father, like daughter. "And suddenly she's able to speak our language."

Greeta turned toward her family, still speaking in Northlander. "I don't understand."

Papa spoke to Greeta while keeping a sharp eye on Thorkel and his daughter.

"You slipped into the Shining Star language. Probably didn't know it when you spoke it."

Thorkel took long strides toward his daughter and clapped a strong arm around her shoulder. "This be my first girl, Frayka."

Frayka crossed her arms, staring at Greeta. "What was that first thing you said to me? That gibberish you spoke."

Greeta hesitated, worried by the way Papa eyed them. But she sensed no reason why she shouldn't tell the truth. "I asked if you were born in the Great Turtle Lands."

"I was born in the Northlands. Not here in the Land of Ice but in the true Northlands." Frayka's words rang sharp and cold.

Thorkel turned his good nature up a notch. "There, there, Frayka. The dragonish girl don't mean nothing harmful. She just be curious is all." Speaking to Greeta, he said, "Frayka's the one who takes after my Grandmum who hailed from the Far East. Frayka's a true Northlander for being born in the Northlands, but her looks come from my Grandmum and the Far

East, along with Frayka's flair for the portents."

"No need to mention that to strangers," Frayka said under her breath. "And I don't appreciate being compared to savages in the Land of Vines."

"Savages?" Greeta said. "What savages?"

"Grandmum told me about it," Thorkel said. "Long ago, she told me about the Land of Vines when I was just a boy. She knew some Northlanders that made the journey across the wide Western Sea. They came back to tell stories of screeching demons in the Land of Vines."

Frayka braced herself as if standing against a howling wind. "They're creatures with feathers in their hair and painted faces. They're monsters that arm themselves with daggers and ax blades made from sharpened stone. They're demons that scream when they cut off men's heads."

Thorkel shuddered. "Scared me something awful in my boyhood."

"But that's nonsense," Greeta said. "I lived all my life in the Great Turtle Lands in a village of the Shining Star nation." She hesitated, remembering how she'd felt hurt by people she'd trusted. But it would not be fair to blame all of the Shining Star people for the unkindness of a few. "They are good people. They're not creatures or monsters or demons."

Frayka considered Greeta for a long moment and then turned to Thorkel. "You called her dragonish. This is the one you say used to be a dragon?"

"When she be little," Thorkel confirmed.

Frayka snorted. "Well, she's not much of a dragon now, is she? That makes her useless. How can these people be any help to us?"

Greeta felt Papa's steady hands on her shoulders as she stiffened with anger. "I am not useless. None of us are useless."

Rognvald's voice boomed behind Greeta. "Ain't that hard a problem."

Turning around, she saw him surrounded by what appeared to be most of the Northlanders in Blackstone, including all the young men and women she'd seen carrying buckets of water from the waterfall.

Rognvald spoke to Frayka with respect, making it clear he considered her his equal. He pointed at Papa. "This man's likely to be the last one alive who knows the secret of making a dragonslayer sword. We need him."

Greeta's eyes widened in wonder. She'd heard Papa talk about such swords before, but he'd never said anything about being the only one who could make them.

Rognvald pointed at Auntie Peppa. "Everyone here says this woman's the best at finding raw iron and smelting it into blooms. The blacksmith can't make swords to slay dragons until his sister gets him the iron he needs."

Surprised again, Greeta looked at Auntie Peppa with raised eyebrows.

Auntie Peppa shrugged. "I'm no better at it than anyone else."

"Shut up," Rognvald said. "Ain't no use in playing modest. We already know the truth. These people here remember when they worked alongside you in the Bog Lands." He looked at Greeta sideways. "We met the girl when she was a dragon baby. Ain't no telling what she is now."

"Useless," Frayka muttered. "I warned you not to bring them here. They can't help. They'll only get in the way. Send them back where they came from."

Rognvald pointed an aggressive finger at her. "Not necessarily. Give the girl a fighting chance."

Frayka crossed her arms and stared at him in defiance.

Sighing, Rognvald pointed at the ocean behind him. "Ain't no one taking her back any time soon. Get used to the girl being here. Show her how to get water. We got matters to discuss."

Thorkel patted his daughter's shoulder and then pushed her toward Greeta. "Rognvald be right. Be a good host while we talk."

"By the gods," Frayka muttered, motioning for Greeta to join her as she walked into Thorkel's stone house.

Greeta followed with caution, not knowing why she felt the need. Stepping into the one-room home, she hesitated from the change of bright sunlight to a dim interior. The hearth fire in the center of the room had dwindled to little more than glowing coals, and the opening in the roof above it let precious little light inside.

Suddenly, she found herself slammed up against the stone wall, its uneven surface painful against her body.

Frayka pinned her with a well-placed forearm under Greeta's chin. "If you want to live," Frayka said, "you'll do exactly what I say."

CHAPTER 5

"What's wrong?" Greeta sputtered, barely able to speak from the force of Frayka's bony forearm against her throat. Frantic, she raised her hands and tried to push Frayka away with no luck. "Why are you doing this?"

Frayka seemed like a monster in the dim light of the stone house, her eyes black and menacing. "I saw you looking at my friends when they came back with water. Don't deny it!"

Greeta struggled to speak. "Yes, I saw them."

"You stared at one of the men. You think you fancy him?"

Trying to swallow, Greeta found she

couldn't. "Please. Let me breathe." Even more frantic, she pushed against Frayka's shoulders.

Easing off, Frayka took a step back. She pulled a dagger from under her belt and held its sharp edge against Greeta's throat. "Better?"

"Much," Greeta said, holding still.

"If you ever look at my man again, I will kill you."

The sharp blade held steady against Greeta's skin. "I didn't know. I promise."

Frayka's eyes flashed in the dim light of the dying fire. "Why does your insincerity cause me doubt?"

"I don't know. But I know what it's like when someone steals the love of your life."

The fierceness in Frayka's eyes softened. "Tell me."

Greeta raised a hand, pushed the dagger aside, and rubbed her neck. "Back home I grew up with a boy. Wapiti. We were friends. Allies. We'd do anything for each other. We talked for years about spending our lives together and having a family of our own." The freshness of the memory raised tears in Greeta's eyes.

Something in the dying fire popped and

fizzled.

"What happened?"

Still rubbing her neck as if that would make her feel better, Greeta said, "My cousin stole him from me. My Auntie Peppa's daughter, Animosh. Even worse, Animosh already has a man of her own and two little children."

Frayka tucked the dagger back under her belt and crossed her arms. "That makes no sense. If she had what she wanted, why want more? Are you sure she stole him? You probably misunderstood."

Mimicking Frayka, Greeta crossed her own arms. "Did you misunderstand when I looked at your man?"

"Of course not, but—"

"They ridiculed me," Greeta said, her voice breaking from the pain of remembering. "I saw them. I heard them. They thought I wasn't there. And my cousin might as well have offered herself to him. My Auntie Peppa confronted them. She told Wapiti that he must honor the wife of a fellow warrior. She told my cousin to take care of her children."

Frayka shifted her weight from one foot to the other, seeming to search for a comfortable stance. "And you?"

"I lost the man I thought would be my closest ally forever."

Frayka nodded. "Good." She turned to the fire and poked at it.

When Greeta spoke, the sharpness in her voice made her glad. "Good? Are you gloating at my sorrow?"

"Of course not." With a few more pokes, Frayka brought the fire back to life. "If you lost him, then you didn't forgive him and take him back. He's a bad man. Your life is better without him." Frayka brushed ashes from her hands. "That's why it's good."

Greeta wanted to argue but couldn't think of anything to say.

"We keep our water buckets here," Frayka said, gesturing to a row of buckets lined up against the wall. Some were filled with water while a few stood empty. "Grab a couple."

Picking up a bucket in each hand, Greeta said, "So you're not going to kill me?"

Frayka picked up her own buckets and stood in the open doorway. "Not as long as you keep your hands off my man." Still blocking the doorway, Frayka looked as dark and deep as a shadow, the sunlight bright behind her. "But tell me something. Did you want to kill your cousin? For what she did?"

Startled by the question, Greeta said, "I would never do such a thing."

"I didn't say did you do it." Frayka's voice sounded as dark as her shadow appearance. "I asked if you wanted to kill her. Doing something and wanting can be two very different things as long as you keep your wits about you." Frayka's voice softened. "Tell me. Did you want to?"

Greeta would never have asked herself such a question and had never thought about it until this moment. She stared at Frayka's silhouette, compelled to give an honest answer. She thought back to the moment she'd first realized her cousin and sweetheart had betrayed her, mulling over the myriad of feelings that had washed through her. "Yes. I wanted to kill her."

Frayka's voice brightened. "Good. You might be a true Northlander despite yourself." She stepped into the bright sunlight, turned to the left, and disappeared.

CHAPTER 6

Greeta hurried out of Thorkel's stone house to follow Frayka toward the waterfall, buckets in hand. Catching up to walk by the Northlander woman's side, Greeta found herself falling into step with her.

"What do you know about the Land of Ice?" Frayka asked.

"Next to nothing."

Frayka stopped abruptly, putting her buckets down. "Then listen close and don't forget what I tell you."

Greeta followed suit by putting her buckets on the ground. "All right."

"Look at the path we're on."

The dirt path stood wide inside Blackstone where they stood. At the edge of the settlement it narrowed, allowing space for two people to walk side by side.

"Now look at the land surrounding the path."

Lush green fields flanked the dirt, stretching to the waterfall and beyond.

"Except for the path," Frayka said, "everything you see is unpredictable. Make no assumptions unless you want to die."

Greeta took a closer look at the grassy fields, but they looked fine. "I don't understand."

"This place shifts and changes all the time."

Greeta paused, remembering what Red Feather had told her about shapeshifters. Remembering that he claimed Greeta was a shapeshifter.

Frayka swept an arm across the horizon. "The ground tears itself apart, but grass grows everywhere: on solid ground and in its crevices, too. This land looks safe, but it is a trap. An innocent step could slide your foot into a shallow crevice, which could break your ankle or your leg. Or you could end up in a deeper chasm, which is like getting swallowed up by the land." Frayka picked up her buckets and began to walk again. "That means stay on the path. No matter what."

Collecting her own buckets, Greeta caught up with her. "So you made these paths? Your people?"

"Father says the paths were here when we arrived. There are paths all around here." Frayka pointed at a hill north of Blackstone. "There's even a path to the hot springs beyond that hill. We go there all the time."

Greeta looked all around. Other than the settlement and sheep grazing in an adjacent field, the land spread far and wide and open. "Other people made them? There are other people who live here?"

Frayka quickened her pace, ignoring Greeta's question.

Falling behind, Greeta examined the path while she walked, considering it might have been made by animals heading to the waterfall to quench their thirst. But the surface of the path was smooth and even, and it had a consistent width that allowed two people to walk next to each other. Paths worn by animals tended to be narrow and bumpy.

People made this path. Either people liv-

ed here before and are gone, or they live in another settlement. But why doesn't Frayka want to admit it? Are there other Northlanders in the Land of Ice? Did they used to be part of this settlement?

Or are they a different kind of people altogether?

When they neared the waterfall, Greeta realized its height and breadth were much grander than what it looked like from a distance. The path ended a short distance from the waterfall, and a series of large, flat stones created a new path leading directly to and all around the pool of water at the base of the fall. A steady stream ran along the base of the cliff, sloping down toward the sea.

Frayka paused long enough to draw her coat-like outermost dress closer around her body, tightening her belt to keep it in place. She shouted to make herself heard over the roar of the crashing water. Pointing ahead, Frayka said, "Stay on the rock path. The ground here can be uncertain."

Frayka led the way, and Greeta stayed close enough on her heels to step where Frayka stepped, noticing some of the large rocks felt solid and stable beneath her feet while others teetered the moment she placed her weight on them. The spray from the fall drenched the surface of the rocks, making them slippery. Greeta took every step with caution and lagged behind Frayka, who walked with confidence and purpose.

Glancing back, Frayka called out, "Don't straggle!"

Greeta shivered, realizing she still wore a buckskin shirt and breeches, which left much of her skin bare. The spray from the waterfall felt clean and pure, unlike the stickiness of the ocean spray that still clung to her skin. Catching up with Frayka, Greeta stood an arm's length from one of the many narrow streams cascading from high above. She copied the way Frayka held each bucket out to capture the water.

Shouldering each bucket, Frayka said, "That's enough. Let's go." She brushed past Greeta, headed toward the path that had brought them here.

Greeta knelt, attempting to draw each heavy bucket up onto her own shoulders as Frayka had done. Realizing too late that she didn't have Frayka's strength, Greeta lost control and each bucket spilled. One fell into the pool of water while the other clattered across the rocks and into the cave behind the waterfall.

The bucket in the pool floated by the edge, but the other bucket threatened to roll out of sight. Mortified at the thought of losing something that not only didn't belong to her but that was likely to be precious and valuable to the people who owned it, Greeta scrambled across the rocks in pursuit of the bucket that rolled away.

Beyond the roar of the waterfall she heard Frayka cry out, "Greeta, no!"

Assuming Frayka worried for her safety, Greeta forged ahead, confident as she stepped from rock to rock until she found an empty space where she could step between the powerful falling streams and into the cave. She hesitated, waiting for her eyes to adjust to the dim light. Somewhere nearby, she heard the clatter of wood against stone slowing to a halt, telling her the bucket must have rolled to a stop. Now all she had to do was find it.

Greeta stretched out her arms, hoping to feel a cave wall to guide her. She found empty air instead. But until her vision adjusted to the darkness of the cave, she didn't dare move.

The falling water behind her shifted, allowing a stream of sunlight to pierce the darkness. The beam landed on the floor to Greeta's left, illuminating a pile of glittering silver next to the bucket that had fallen and rolled away from her.

Greeta walked alongside the stream of light, taking every step on the uneven cave floor with care. Kneeling to gather the bucket, she stared at the pile of silver: arm bands, rings, brooches.

A shadow broke the beam of light, but enough time had passed to allow Greeta to see in the dimness. Looking up, she saw Frayka's dark silhouette standing between her and the falling water.

"You weren't supposed to see that," Frayka said.

CHAPTER 7

"What is this?" Greeta said, looking back at the pile of silver hidden inside the cave. "Where did it come from?"

"None of your business," Frayka said, her voice harsh and strained. "Pick up that bucket. I've got the other one you dropped. Get more water and go."

Since arriving in the Land of Ice, Greeta had felt intimidated by Frayka, especially because Frayka had no doubts about being accepted by her people even though she looked nothing like them. Greeta had lost that confidence back home when the people she loved betrayed and humiliated her.

Although Frayka appeared to be warming up ever-so-slightly, Greeta wondered whether she could trust her. Frayka seemed like someone who needed to be in charge at all costs, and that made Greeta feel uneasy. She wanted to feel more like Frayka's equal and less like her servant girl.

Now she'd discovered something Frayka wanted to keep secret, and Greeta decided to use it to her own advantage. "This silver must be yours. But your father doesn't know about it?"

Frayka's tone took a harder edge. "Like I said, it's none of your business."

That means her father doesn't know! From the way Frayka is acting, she doesn't want him to know.

Because I know something she doesn't want her father to know, I finally have some power over her.

Greeta sat next to the pile of silver, making herself comfortable. "I think it's become my business. This is quite a hoard. I've never seen so much wealth in my life." She held a ring up in the beam of light that still illuminated the treasure, making sure that Frayka saw her slip the ring on her finger.

Frayka stalked toward her, pointing at the ring. "That's not yours! Take it off!"

"I'm just borrowing it." Greeta smiled sweetly. "I think I'll wear it back to your house and show everyone."

Frayka leapt to grab her hand, but Greeta balled it up in a fist and rolled away. Frayka stumbled and fell to the ground but scrambled back to her feet.

"I'm just curious about where and how you acquired all this," Greeta said. "I won't tell anyone."

And if I can convince you to tell me, then I'll know even more that you don't want your father to know. We'll be on even footing. You won't be able to boss me around.

"Give it to me or I'll punch you in the face."

"And how will you explain that to my family?" Greeta kept smiling. "The people your father brought here because he needs their help?"

Frayka glared at Greeta and growled in frustration. Finally, she plopped on the ground, sitting next to her. "Fine. What do you want?"

"I told you. I'm curious about where this came from."

Frayka's dark eyes glinted, reflecting the light streaming into the cave. "You can't tell anyone. Not your father. Not your aunt. Not anyone. Not ever."

Greeta took off the ring and handed it to Frayka. "I promise."

Frayka sighed as if she were shouldering not only her own buckets full of water but Greeta's as well. "Father and the other men have been taking their ship to the islands south of here when the weather allows."

"Islands?"

Frayka nodded. "There's a stretch of islands far off the coast of the Northlands."

Greeta's heart began to race. "Why do they go there?"

"For trading. Like they did in the old days. Before the Northlands and the Midlands and the Southlands were destroyed. The islands fared better, and some people still live there."

"But this is your silver, not something your father brought back. How did you get it?"

Frayka stared at her hands as if still considering whether or not punching Greeta would be worth the repercussions.

"Weeks ago they brought back a second ship. One they traded for. When Father sailed off for the Land of Vines, some of us took the other ship to go trading on our own." Frayka paused and cleared her throat. "But after we traded on the islands, we sailed to the shore of the Northlands to see what it was like. We've all heard stories. We wanted to see for ourselves."

Greeta's heart beat even faster, convinced that the answer to how and why she had turned into a dragon had to be somewhere in the Northlands, the former home of her family and the place where she'd been born. "What did you see?"

"This." Frayka pointed at the silver. "We found some old deserted homes and found this."

"Why do you hide it?"

"Because we're forbidden to go anywhere near the Northlands. They say it's too dangerous."

"Are you going to go again?"

Frayka nodded. "Sometime before the days grow short and the seas become too rough."

"Take me with you. If you don't, I'll tell

your father where you've been and what you found."

Reluctantly, Frayka nodded her acceptance of Greeta's demand.

CHAPTER 8

A week later Greeta stood in the smithery at the edge of Blackstone. She had
ditched her old clothes in exchange for the
same type of dress that the other Northlander women wore. Except for today, because Papa had advised that long skirts in
a smithery could too easily catch fire.
Once again, Greeta wore men's apparel:
brightly colored pants and a shirt with
sleeves rolled up above the elbow. She felt
peculiar wearing men's clothes, but she
kept telling herself it would only be for her
brief time in the smithery. Then she could
go back to looking like a woman again.

Papa promised that after her time in the
smithery, Greeta could join the young

Northlander women who had promised to take her to the hot springs just beyond the settlement, where they could all ease their tired bodies in soothing water.

And after that, Greeta and her family would sail home to their Shining Star village in the Great Turtle Lands.

More and more her thoughts wandered to Red Feather. Greeta felt convinced he'd seen the Northlander ship sail away from the beach back home. She wondered what Red Feather had thought. Did he understand she'd been taken against her will? Or did he think she'd deserted their people on a whim?

Greeta shook those thoughts away. It seemed peculiar to spend so much time thinking about the brother of the man she'd loved her whole life.

Papa argued with Thorkel and Rognvald. Papa crossed his arms and told them, "Won't work. Never agreed to that."

Greeta had never seen Papa like this before. Back home he acted happy and relaxed most of the time, getting along peaceably with all Shining Star people as well as his own family. With iron being scarce in the Great Turtle Lands, he'd given up blacksmithing and taken charge of growing crops for the Shining Star village.

Knowing how much he missed blacksmithing, Greeta had assumed he'd be even happier here among Northlanders. Instead, they'd succeeded in confounding and irritating her father.

Rognvald pointed an accusing finger at the high stone wall that separated the smithery from Blackstone.

Greeta knew the Northlanders had built this wall many years ago to provide the smithery with a wind block from the shore. But then she noticed another advantage: the wall also hid the smithery from any prying eyes in Blackstone. Papa had made it clear that the technique for making dragonslayer swords had to be kept secret.

"Ain't no reason to complain," Rognvald said. "That wall give you all the secrecy you demand."

"Don't tell men they can work with me," Papa said. "I choose who I work with. Not you."

"And if we give no men to help?" Thorkel leaned against the wall. "How long it be to make a dragonish sword with your hands alone?"

Papa gazed up at the sun, high in the sky. "With so much daylight, perhaps a week."

The days were longer in the Land of Ice. The sun drifted to the horizon late at night and merely rested upon it for a short time instead of setting. Instead of pitch black night, the light merely dimmed for several hours. Greeta found it difficult to sleep and yet felt full of energy all the time.

"And if you had men helping you?" Rognvald said.

Papa shrugged. "A few days."

"So take our men and teach them!" Rognvald said. "Make all the swords you can. As fast as you can!"

Greeta rested one hand on top of the anvil, fascinated by its smooth surface and cool touch. She gazed at the array of tools laid out on the table, shielded from the elements by a metal canopy overhead. She drifted to the blacksmithing fire and used a metal poker to stir the flames and keep them going while the men argued.

"A proper sword takes time and careful making." Papa spoke firmly, keeping his temper even. "No use in making swords fast if they end up bending or breaking. Rushing a sword is the worst thing for it."

"He be wanting the proper kind of help," Thorkel said to Rognvald. "Not any kind of help we can offer."

"Ain't going to have what we need if he don't work fast," Rognvald said. He paced, looking at the rocky plains beyond Blackstone. "Weren't that the whole point of bringing him here? To get swords before we set up the fortifications before winter?"

Greeta kept her eyes on the fire and kept prodding it. But Rognvald's words held her spellbound. Frayka and her friends wouldn't set sail while their fathers were in the settlement. But once the days grew shorter, the men would journey inland to erect a barrier made of trees, felled and sharpened, forming a large boundary around Blackstone to detain the ice dragons that the Northlanders claimed would attack when the weather turned cold. That journey would take several days.

Frayka and the other young women and men of Blackstone had promised to fish in the deep seas during that journey, just as they had done when the elders had sailed to fetch Greeta's family. And they'd succeeded in bringing back a wealth of fish. They hadn't mentioned they'd also gone trading (and had traded for the fish instead of catching them) and ventured onto the shores of the Northlands.

"One proper sword is better than an armful of useless ones," Papa said. "I make swords in my way and time or not at all."

"See?" Thorkel said to Rognvald. "I told you so."

Rognvald ground his teeth. "Don't come complaining to me when the ice dragons bite off your head and spit it into the ocean." He stomped back toward the settlement.

Following, Thorkel said, "Don't see how I could complain if my head's bitten off. Never saw a man cut off from his head complain about anything before."

After Papa watched them disappear behind the wall, he turned and smiled at the sight of Greeta minding the fire. "Want to learn how to make a sword?"

Her own leaping heart surprised Greeta. "But you won't teach the Northlander men. Why would you teach me?"

"You're family." Papa searched among

the tools, picking up a few different hammers and weighing them in his hands. "Like I told you before, there's a secret to making swords for dragonslayers. It's kept within families, passed down from generation to generation." Looking up at Greeta, he said, "Thorkel and Rognvald may be right. It could be that me and Peppa are the last ones who know it. It's time for you to learn so one more of us knows it."

Greeta turned her back to the fire. "Why keep it secret?"

A rustling of footsteps in the grass made them both turn to look at the wall shielding them from Blackstone and any prying eyes.

"Don't worry." Auntie Peppa beamed, rounding the end of the wall and clutching a lumpy sack to her chest as if it were full of precious gems. "It's just me."

Greeta didn't realize her entire body had tensed until she felt it relax.

Auntie Peppa walked up to the table and dumped the contents of her sack onto it.

Rocks. Why has Peppa brought rocks to us?

Auntie Peppa laughed, nudging her brother and pointing at Greeta. "How can you call yourself a blacksmith when your own daughter can't tell a bloom of iron from a mud pie?"

"These are blooms of iron?" Greeta picked one up and turned it over in her hand. The bloom filled her palm and had a good heft. Taking a closer look at its dark color, she finally recognized it as metal.

"Smelted this morning," Auntie Peppa said. Turning to Papa, she said, "They have nothing like the bogs in the North-lands. But in the years they've been here, they've discovered a field of black rocks by a trench the size of a lake. Looks as if the earth itself spit them out. If you look close enough, you can find decent lumps of iron among those black rocks."

Papa shook his head in wonder, picking up an especially large bloom and turning it over in his hands. "Why should it be so easy to find iron in this part of the world and so hard back home?"

Auntie Peppa nudged him again. "You were telling your child about the secret." Before he could ask, she said, "Don't worry. Everyone else is back at Blackstone. There are no eavesdroppers here."

Nodding his understanding, Papa showed the bloom he held to Greeta. "Most blacksmiths would make a sword from this. Big enough for one blade when you hammer it out. That's the problem."

Greeta frowned. "The problem?"

Papa tossed the bloom in the air and caught it with his other hand. "You can't know its character until it's too late."

Baffled, Greeta said, "Character?"

"Just like people," Auntie Peppa said. "Sometimes you think you know someone, and then they surprise you. They're not the person you thought they were."

Auntie Peppa's words felt like a dagger through Greeta's heart. It had only been weeks since Wapiti, her childhood sweetheart, had betrayed her. Greeta had spent her life believing they'd someday be married and have a family, only to see him switch his loyalty to her married cousin just because that cousin flirted with him.

Seeming to understand Greeta's sudden discomfort, Auntie Peppa's voice softened. "Like people, the true character of each and every bloom of iron is hidden deep within. Even after it's forged into a weapon or nails or a plow blade, you can't predict its character. It's only with time that you discover whether it's weak or strong. If the iron's character is weak, it will bend or even break in time. But if it's strong, the iron holds its forged shape, never bending or breaking."

Greeta couldn't help but think of Red Feather, Wapiti's oldest brother. Red Feather had been a true and loyal friend to Greeta. He'd been what she wished Wapiti could be.

"That's the trouble with making a sword from one bloom," Papa said. "There you could be, in the middle of fighting a dragon, and what happens? Your blade breaks in two and the dragon has you for its supper."

Auntie Peppa took the large bloom of iron away from Papa and put it back on the table. "But there's a secret to making swords for dragonslayers. These swords will never bend or break. They're the most powerful weapons a blacksmith can make."

Greeta stared at the blooms of iron spread out on the table, ranging in size from the large one that had filled Papa's hand to blooms half its size. "But how?"

Papa picked out a few of the smallest blooms and piled them on his open hand. "Use different blooms to make one sword. Hammer them into billets, which look a bit like spindles. You twist those billets around each other. Forge them together into a single blade."

"Some blooms will be weak in character," Auntie Peppa said. "That gives the sword flexibility."

"Others are strong, giving it strength," Papa said. "A sword that's strong but flexible, that won't bend or break. That's the kind of sword you want when you're facing a dragon."

His words chilled Greeta. She heard the strain in her own voice when she spoke. "The swords are for killing dragons. Dragons like me?"

"Oh, Greeta," Auntie Peppa said. "We don't mean you. Remember how we told you there are two types of dragons? The dragons that need to be killed are like rogue bears that kill people. You're not like that."

"Dragons are like iron," Papa said. "But their character isn't weak or strong. It's good or bad. There were bad dragons in the world, ones that killed people."

"We had to have dragonslayers," Auntie Peppa said. "Or the bad dragons would kill entire villages or destroy people's crops, leaving them to starve to death. And these dragons were pure animal. They weren't shapeshifters."

Greeta still felt uneasy but at the same time encouraged that her family revealed more information she needed to understand. Questions swarmed in her head like moon flies, but she didn't want to ask too much. The sooner they could finish making swords, the sooner she'd be home. "How did dragonslayers know whether or not to kill a dragon? How could they tell the difference between a good and a bad dragon?"

Papa shrugged. "Don't know. I just make the swords. And considering your mother showed me how to make a dragonslayer's sword, it seems high time I teach you to do the same. Just remember to keep it secret."

"Why?" Greeta said. "If this is the best way to make a sword, why not use it for all swords? Not just to make swords for dragonslayers but for everyday people?"

Papa and Auntie Peppa exchanged a worried look.

"Because people are like dragons," Papa said. "Some are bad. If they learn how to make a dragonslayer's sword, they'll use it against the good people. That's why we keep it secret. To keep good people safe."

"The Northlanders in Blackstone," Greeta said. "Aren't they good people? Couldn't you trust them with the secret?"

Papa cast a long look at Greeta. "Most likely. You never dangle temptation in front of anyone, including good people. The secret is temptation that could turn good people bad." He pointed at the wall separating them from Blackstone. "But they're in need of swords better than what they've got. *That* I'm willing to give them." Winking at Greeta, Papa said, "Ready to help?"

CHAPTER 9

While Auntie Peppa kept guard to make sure no Northlanders let their curiosity get the better of them, Greeta watched Papa build a fire in a trench, put the blooms of iron in it, bring those blooms to a proper heat, and then forge them. The way the iron changed color from black to dull red to glowing orange to bright yellow startled and fascinated Greeta, making her feel a kinship with the iron because of its ability to change shape and color.

She marveled at Papa's ease with the blacksmithing tools. Under his command, each bloom of iron changed shape so quickly and easily that it seemed like magic. Even though each bloom held its color and heat for a few blinks of an eye, Papa made good use of that time and hammered the bloom into something different by the time he put it back in the fire. Because he kept several blooms in the same fire, one was always ready for smiting.

Papa encouraged Greeta to do more than watch, teaching her how to handle the tools and keep the anvil swept clean of slag, flakes of weakness that emerged from iron after every blow.

By the time the sun skimmed along the horizon, Papa had forged each bloom into a long rod of iron he'd use to make the sword. Now Greeta understood why he'd made the fire in a trench: it was long and wide enough to put the rods side-by-side in the fire.

Auntie Peppa had paced between this private smithery and Blackstone all day, hauling water and food for Papa and Greeta. She now stared at the horizon. "Do we sleep here for the night?"

Papa laughed. "We still got daylight. But you go home if you like, Peppa. Doubt no one will trouble us tonight."

Nodding, Auntie Peppa bid them good night and walked toward Blackstone, disappearing behind the wall.

"You want to work through the night?" Greeta said, astonished by the idea.

Papa shrugged. "Don't see why not. It'll be twilight all night. Between that and the fire, there's plenty of light. We can get a rough sword welded together by morning and then take a few days to finish it." He handed a pair of tongs to Greeta. "Why don't you take a try at twisting a rod?"

Terror and delight filled Greeta at the same time. "But I don't know how. What if I ruin it?"

Papa pulled a straight rod out of the fire. He'd built the fire and created the trench so that he could heat sections of each rod at a time, leaving part of the rod black and cold. He gripped the black end with his own tongs and placed it on the anvil. "I'll show you how." With one hand he held the rod in place against the anvil. With the other, he used tongs to grasp a section and twist it quickly several times until the rod had a twist the length of Greeta's hand at one end. "We twist each one in different places," Papa said. "You want each rod to be straight, twisted, straight, twisted, straight, twisted, but just spinning the twist so the rod itself stays straight as a blade." He returned the rod to the fire and pulled out another one. Placing it on the anvil, he said, "You try."

Greeta knew she couldn't hesitate. Otherwise, the heat allowing her to shape the iron would be gone. Greeta grabbed the bright yellow end with her tongs and did the best she could to copy what Papa had done. But the metal didn't move as easily and fluidly as it did under her father's strong grasp. It barely twisted at all.

"Put your mind and your shoulder into it," Papa said.

Taking his advice, Greeta concentrated and threw her body into twisting the iron, this time turning it better and faster. But by the time the bright yellow had cooled to orange, the metal stubbornly resisted her force. She backed away from the anvil to find her twist looked like an ugly, uneven contortion instead of her father's beautiful work. "I ruined it. It looks horrible!"

Papa put the rod back into the fire. "Nonsense. You gave it character. That twist will give it a special pattern."

"You're not going to fix it?" Greeta said. "Won't it damage the sword? Make it weak?"

"Shouldn't." Papa pulled out the next rod, gesturing to Greeta to hold it in place on the anvil while he twisted it. "Twisting gives it a pattern. What matters is the different blooms of iron we forge into billets, not how you twist the billets."

Greeta frowned, watching her father work with strength and swiftness. His twists were uniform and perfect. "It won't be as pretty."

Papa laughed, glancing up to meet her gaze. "Plenty of worse things in life than a sword not as pretty as some others."

They worked through the night. The sun seemed to keep them energized. Sometimes the sun appeared to rest on the horizon. Other times it dipped slightly below the horizon only to peek above it a short time later.

By the time the sun began to climb in the sky, Papa had forged all the billets together into the rough shape of a blade standing as tall as Greeta's shoulder. All of the Northlanders carried daggers tucked their belts. The dagger blades were thin and polished, not coarse and dull like this one. And each dagger had a grip that allowed its owner to hold onto the weapon. The sword Papa had forged had no grip and was nothing but blade. "I don't understand," Greeta said. "How can anyone hold onto this?"

"That comes last," Papa said. He pointed at a narrow tail jutting out at the opposite end from the sword's point. "Here's the tang. We hammer the sword into shape and finish it up. We take care of the tang last. We make a crossguard and thread it over the tang. We push the crossguard to rest against the top of the blade. Put a pommel on the end of the tang. Wrap up the rest of the tang with leather to make a grip. And then the sword's done." Handing the sword to her, he said, "Get a feel for holding it."

Greeta put both hands on the raw tang, holding the sword straight in front of her and parallel to the ground.

Papa took a step back in surprise. "You got your mama's instincts. How else can you know the way to grip a sword when you never seen one before?"

Greeta realized she hadn't told anyone about her walks in the Dreamtime back in the Great Turtle Lands. Maybe she'd been questioning how real they'd been without realizing it. But now all the training she'd had with Margreet came rushing back. In the Dreamtime, she'd trained first with wooden versions of swords and then with real iron. She hesitated, not sure if the time had come to talk to Papa about having learned to walk in the Dreamtime and what she'd experienced there.

Before she could decide, shouts pierced the air on the other side of the wall separating the smithery from the Northlanders' settlement.

Papa pulled the dagger from where he kept it tucked underneath his belt and ran around one corner of the wall, only to stop short, bewildered.

Holding onto the rough sword, Greeta ran to join his side.

CHAPTER 10

Greeta ran to her father's side, startled and confused by what she saw on the other side of the wall separating the smithery from Blackstone.

All the Northlanders rushed to the opposite side of the settlement, where three small hills of ice had appeared.

Greeta recognized ice when she saw it. The winters in her region of the Great Turtle Lands tended to be long and harsh, although nothing like what she'd heard about the winters here in the Land of Ice. In her Shining Star village, streams of fresh water would turn to ice. Snow fell for weeks. Her people often depended on collecting snow and melting it as their water supply throughout the winter. During especially harsh seasons, the ocean would sweep chunks of ice as large as houses to the shore and deposit them on the frozen sand.

Not knowing what she saw in the distance, Greeta tried to make sense of it. Is that what had happened here? Had some wayward ice been swept in by the ocean?

But how could that be when they were a good walking distance from the beach of black sand?

Cracking, splitting sounds filled the air, and the mounds of ice moved.

"Ice dragons," Papa whispered.

Greeta looked at him, startled to see the color drain from his face.

"Stay here, Greeta. Hide!" Clutching his dagger, Papa sprinted toward Blackstone.

Weeks ago, Greeta would have obeyed him without question and hid behind the wall. But that was before she had walked in the Dreamtime or changed into a dragon. Something had shifted inside her. Something that made her abandon fear.

Tucking the rough sword under her arm, Greeta ran, following her father's footsteps.

Within moments Greeta found herself in the thick of the settlement, surrounded by the cries of children inside the small stone homes.

Men and women dashed to collect the most convenient weapon at hand: stones or buckets or trowels from the garden. Greeta gained a deeper understanding for their need for Papa to make swords, remembering she'd only seen Thorkel and Rognvald carry weapons larger than the daggers everyone else kept on hand. Once armed, they raced ahead toward the commotion.

Steps later, Greeta almost ran headlong into Frayka, calm as the eye of a storm, while the young man she claimed was hers shouted at her.

"This is your fault!" the handsome young man shouted, jabbing an accusing finger at Frayka. "You brought this upon us. You made it happen!"

"I only read the portents," Frayka said, standing straight and tall. "I told you this would happen, Njall. I told everyone. I did it so we wouldn't be taken by surprise." Pulling the knife from her belt, Frayka hiked up her skirts with the other hand,

brushed past the young man, and ran toward the direction of the fight.

"You're a freak!" Njall shouted at her.
"Frayka the freak!" But then he spotted an
ax leaning against a nearby stone house
and took it, running after Frayka.

Following his lead, Greeta scanned the
grounds: the stone homes clustered close
together within Blackstone, the worn dirt
paths between them, and the last few
Northlanders running past her. Seeing nothing left behind that could serve as a
weapon, Greeta kept the unfinished sword
clutched under her arm and followed
them.

Dozens of Northlanders stood at the
edge of Blackstone, all waving their weapons and shouting. Running into the thick
of them, Greeta stared wide-eyed at the
three ice dragons standing a stone's throw
away.

Each towered as high as a ship's mast,
made of chunks of white ice that were polished and bright as gemstones, gleaming
in the sunlight. The chunks seemed to
float against each other like muscles held
together with invisible sinew. Their tails
were like necklaces of ice, whipping back

and forth across the ground. Their eyes glowed like blue fire. When they opened their jaws full of icicle teeth and roared, their frosty breath chilled Greeta's bones.

"Away with you!" shouted Rognvald, waving a short sword.

Standing by his side, Thorkel jabbed his own sword at the ice dragons. "Leave us be!"

The ice dragons edged a step closer, stomping their feet hard enough to make the ground shudder.

Greeta took the unfinished sword from beneath her arm, holding on as well as she could to the tang. Remembering what she'd learned from Margreet in the Dream-time, Greeta held the sword vertical and kept it close to her chest. This way, she could bring it down in a forward blow quickly if need be. Otherwise, holding it this way made the sword feel as light as a feather and easier to grip.

A sudden movement caught Greeta's attention. Looking away from the ice dragons, she saw Frayka edge to the far side of the Northlanders and cross the invisible line separating them from the strange creatures.

What is she doing?

Taking a quick glance at the crowd of Northlanders surrounding her, Greeta realized no one else noticed Frayka slipping around the side because they were so intently focused on the ice dragons facing them.

An ethereal voice whispered in Greeta's ear.

Follow her.

Greeta wasn't sure if the voice was Greeta's own inner good sense or belonged to Margreet, the ghost of the woman after which Greeta had been named. In either case, Greeta knew she had to act and do it quickly.

The ice dragons took another step closer, stomping the ground even harder this time, and it trembled terribly.

Greeta ran sideways through the crowd, pushing through the Northlanders until she broke free and found herself a few steps behind Frayka.

Now in line with the ice dragons but far enough to the side to stay out of their grasp, Frayka held her dagger high above her head and shouted, "Be gone with you!"

All three ice dragons turned their heads

and gazed at her with their fire-blue eyes, their eye sockets soft and melting like tears. The dragons roared and pounded their feet against the ground.

This time, the earth cracked as loud as a lightning strike, splitting open at the invisible line between the Northlanders and the ice dragons. The Northlanders cried out, tumbling to the ground from the force of the tremor.

Greeta fell only to one knee. She regained her balance and stood, still holding onto the unfinished sword with both hands. Finding herself at the edge of a chasm as narrow as her hand, she looked up to see Frayka on the other side, alone with the ice dragons.

The ground roared, and the chasm widened.

Follow her!

Without hesitation, Greeta dashed away from the still-widening chasm and then ran at it with all her might, leaping when she reached the edge.

CHAPTER 11

Greeta leapt across the chasm created by the ice dragons, but it continued to widen. When she reached the other side, it had moved too far for her foot to land on the ground. Instead, she fell and her hips hit the ledge. Reaching forward, she let the momentum of her leap carry her upper body to fold across the ledge and onto solid ground. Letting go of the sword, she saw it fly beyond her grasp and land safely. Her hands clenched fistfuls of grass.

"Greeta!" she heard Papa call from the other side of the chasm.

Glancing back, she saw the Northlanders on the other side of the chasm struggling to their feet. But the chasm had already widened to the length of a ship. Any-one who tried to jump across it now would fall into the depths of the enormous fis-sure.

Greeta dug her feet into the fresh wall of the chasm, feeling the earth crumble be-neath her shoes. Finding a brief foothold, she hauled her body over the ledge and onto the grass.

"Greeta, stay safe!" Papa called. "We're coming to get you!"

With the ground still rumbling and shuddering beneath her, Greeta shouted, "No!" On hands and knees she scrambled forward, finding where her sword had landed and picking it up. Standing, she turned to see Frayka nearby, surrounded by the three ice dragons and slashing at the air between them with her dagger. All of the ice dragons stood on their hind legs, towering over Frayka.

Dimly aware of all the Northlanders now shouting on the other side, everything Greeta learned in the Dreamtime came rushing back. The sword she held in her hands might be unfinished with dull edges, a dull point, and too much heft, but it was still a sword.

Holding the sword high above her head, Greeta rushed toward the nearest ice dragon, fixated on Frayka and the large slashes she made in the air with her dagger. When Greeta reached that ice dragon, she inverted the sword and brought it straight down to impale the ice dragon's foot. Despite the sword's blunt point and rough finish, it pierced the dragon's foot, shattering most of it into shards and impaling what remained to the ground.

Crying out in pain, the ice dragon swung its attention away from Frayka and toward its own impaled foot. The foot wriggled but the sword held it in place. The ice dragon roared at Greeta, its icicle teeth glistening sharp while it blasted her with arctic breath. Wrenching its leg free from the captured foot, the ice dragon stumbled back a few steps toward the chasm.

Greeta yanked the sword free and charged toward the off-balance dragon. She plunged her weapon into its other foot, again impaling it to the ground.

Shocked by the pain, the ice dragon lunged toward Greeta.

She let go of the sword and ran toward the edge of the chasm, now as wide as the settlement behind it.

The ice dragon twisted to follow Greeta's change in direction only to lose control of its balance. Falling to the ground, its shoulder hit the edge of the chasm, and the dragon's body of ice chunks broke apart like shattered glass. Its upper body fell into the chasm. The dragon's roar echoed while it descended deeper and deeper into the fissure. The rest of its body scattered like chunks of ice tossed upon the shore by the sea.

Greeta wrestled the sword out of the ice dragon's severed foot.

Once freed, that chunk of ice shuddered and hopped toward Greeta, seeming to want to fight her in an act of vengeance for what she had done to the rest of its body.

Again, Greeta headed toward the edge of the chasm, letting the foot hop after her. When it came close, she dodged out of its path. In mid-hop, the foot's forward momentum forced it to fall into the abyss.

Seeing the remaining two ice dragons close in on Frayka, Greeta ran toward them, holding her sword high above her head again.

This time the ice dragons noticed her,

dropping down on all fours and baring their icicle teeth at her.

Greeta pulled up short, resting the blade of the unfinished sword on her shoulder to adjust her grip. This time she stepped toward one dragon's jaw, swinging a sideways blow at it with all her might. But the force of the blow caused the sword to fly out of her hands, slightly grazing the dragon's head before falling to the ground.

Stunned, Greeta stared at the sword. It shouldn't have flown out of her hands.

I lost control of it because it's unfinished! A real sword would have a pommel on the end to keep my hands from sliding off.

The dragon swiped her with its icy paw, sending Greeta flying across the grass and landing near the creature's tail.

"Fool!" Frayka shouted at her. "Leave me be!"

Greeta spotted her sword, and scrambled on her hands and feet toward it. Gripping the raw tang, she stood, her mind racing to think of another way to use it.

But then Frayka cried out and darted between the two ice dragons. She sprinted away from the chasm and took a wide swing to the right before disappearing over a low hill.

The ice dragons hesitated, splitting their attention between Frayka, who threatened to disappear from sight, and Greeta, who stood by with sword in hand. Turning their backs on Greeta with disregard, they galloped after Frayka.

Once again tucking the sword under her arm, Greeta remembered what Frayka told her when they fetched water from the waterfall: the land is full of hidden fissures that can twist an ankle or swallow people whole.

Everything you see is unpredictable. Make no assumptions unless you want to die. This place shifts and changes all the time.

The Northlanders still shouted behind her. Turning back, Greeta saw the chasm was now the size of a great wide river, stretching as far as the horizon on each side of Blackstone. She saw no way to return to it. Their voices became quiet until she heard Papa calling again. "Stay there, Greeta. We will find a way to reach you."

First, Greeta felt relief. She wanted to go home. She wanted to be with her family in a familiar and safe place. She knew Papa and the Northlanders would find a way to bring her across the chasm. But then Greeta remembered what the Shining Star people had taught her: to think about how any decision will impact the next seven generations before making that decision.

What will happen to Frayka if I don't follow her?

Frayka had called her a fool and run away in pursuit of the ice dragons.

What if she disappears by the time anyone can help me? What if the ice dragons kill her? What if she gets lost?

Greeta gazed across the chasm but didn't see Thorkel. She didn't know if he felt proud of his daughter for chasing after the ice dragons or fearful for her life.

What will happen if Frayka dies?

Thinking about that possibility made Greeta's heart weigh heavy with the grief she knew Thorkel, his family, and the other Northlanders would feel. In addition to their grief, there might be more far-reaching consequences.

Will Thorkel and the other Northlanders be angry with me for turning my back on her? Will they blame us? Will they also blame the Shining Star nation because we live there?

Frayka had commanded that Greeta leave her be. But that didn't mean abandoning Frayka was the right thing to do.

Am I a coward by not helping Frayka? Am I weak for wanting only what I want instead of helping others in need? What if Frayka dies because I won't help? What if people in Blackstone are hurt because she dies? Will the next seven generations resent the Shining Star nation because I act like a coward?

Could it result in war many years from now when there could have been peace instead?

"Stay there," Papa called again. "Don't move."

"No!" Greeta shouted back across the chasm. She wanted to wait for rescue, but she couldn't bear what her cowardice might lead to in the far future. She wasn't willing to take the slightest risk that her failure to act today could someday be the cause of disharmony or even war. How could anyone live with such shame and guilt? She would make sure Frayka lived and then find a way to return to Blackstone. "There's no time!"

Before Papa or anyone else in Blackstone could answer, Greeta ran in the wake of the ice dragons. The great weight of their icy bodies left footprints in the grass, and Greeta took care to step where they stepped.

The Land of Ice had failed once to swallow her whole. She didn't dare give it a second chance.

CHAPTER 12

Because Greeta took care to watch where she placed every step in order to a-void falling into a hidden crevice, she lag-ged behind Frayka and the two ice dra-gons that hunted her. Unused to running, she felt her chest tighten and struggled for breath. Each footprint left by an ice dra-gon in the grass showed Greeta where she could step with safety, and she hopped from footprint to footprint until she spot-ted a path. Jumping onto it, she followed that path up a hill.

When she reached the crest of the hill, she saw Frayka running around a wide pool of water, its surface foggy with steam.

The hot springs!

Greeta knelt, holding onto her unfinished sword. Now she understood why Frayka had said to let her be. Frayka must have had this plan in mind from the moment she hurled herself across the chasm the ice dragons had created at the edge of Blackstone.

Frayka had run to the opposite end of the hot springs and now waved her dagger. "I'm here! Come and get me!"

That's it, Frayka! Trick them into walking into the hot springs!

Instead, the two ice dragons split up: one circled around one side of the hot springs while the other walked on the opposite side. Before long they would have Frayka cornered.

Worried, Greeta crept down the hill, weapon in hand.

When the ice dragons neared Frayka, she threw her dagger aside, hitched up her skirts, and jumped into the hot springs.

The sight of Frayka vanishing below the steaming water's surface frightened Greeta into thinking the young woman had drowned. The ice dragons stared at the water, seeming to wonder the same thing.

RESA NELSON

Guilt washed through Greeta. Why couldn't she have saved Frayka? Why couldn't Greeta have sent all three ice dragons tumbling to their deaths in the chasm instead of just the one?

Frayka's head bobbed up in the center of the large hot springs. Once again she called out, "I'm here! Come and get me!"

One ice dragon roared, its breath fogging over the hot springs. It plunged into the springs, splashing hot water onto its companion still standing on solid ground. Both dragons cried out in pain.

The dragon on dry ground backed away from the springs, staring at its own body, partially melted and dripping.

The other ice dragon whipped its head frantically as it struggled to walk through the water toward Frayka. The hot water hissed, melting the creature's lower body more and more with every step it took. Steam thickened around it, while the dragon sank deeper until only its head remained above water.

Greeta's guilt dissolved when she noticed her sense of smell sharpen. A slight breeze carried the acrid tang of Frayka's fear and anger. Breathing deeper, Greeta inhaled the chilly presence of the dragons, smelling of focus and determination. In that moment, Greeta felt like a predator in search of prey.

Certain she could handle the other ice dragon on her own, Greeta continued her way down the hill, careful not to draw its attention away from the hot springs.

"That's it!" Frayka shouted at the ice dragon closing in on her, slogging its way through the water. At the same time, Frayka glided toward the opposite end of the hot springs, away from both dragons. "Don't let me get away."

Still climbing down the hill, Greeta circled behind the standing dragon, seeing how she could follow the hill's slope to end up near its thrashing tail. She held onto her sword so tightly that the pressure whitened her hands. She knew she couldn't risk losing the sword again by leting it fly out of her hands. Without a pommel, she couldn't swing and hold onto it at the same time. But she could hold onto the tang with both hands and bring it straight down toward the ground like she'd done to impale the first dragon's foot.

I can do that again with the last ice dragon.

Creeping up behind it, Greeta took care to stay clear of its tail, which trembled while the dragon examined the front part of its body still melting from being splashed with hot water from the springs. When the dragon looked at Frayka and roared its dismay, Greeta took the opportunity to run to its foot and slam the rough point of her sword through it.

But instead of impaling it, the sword shattered the foot, causing the ice dragon to sink to the stump of its leg.

Shocked, the creature turned its attention away from Frayka and toward Greeta.

Holding on tight to her sword, Greeta dashed around the side of the hot springs, heading toward the other end that Frayka had nearly reached.

The ice dragon snapped its jaws at her, trying to run only to limp instead. It paused, studying its stump and then looking back at the remnants of the foot that had been shattered.

Greeta reversed direction and ran toward the ice dragon again, this time bringing her sword down through the dragon's other foot. The sword pierced the ice and impaled the dragon's remaining good foot to the ground.

Enraged, the ice dragon turned to see Greeta run away. When it tried to give chase, it fell, causing the ground to shudder.

Greeta hesitated at the sensation of the earth trembling beneath her.

What if another chasm opens up? I can't be separated from Frayka!

But hadn't she also felt the ground tremble just moments before she turned into a dragon back in the Great Turtle Lands?

What if it has nothing to do with another chasm opening up? What if I turn into a dragon again?

The wind carried the warmth of steam, which filled her nostrils and made her nose twitch. Greeta thought she tasted the ice dragon's anger, and it made the back of her tongue burn.

I need to be a dragon now! I can destroy the ice dragons by myself.

Greeta's skin itched with such intensity that it made her wish she could crawl out of it.

She waited for her dragon body to burst through her clothing, but nothing happened. Greeta closed her eyes and tried to force herself to become a dragon, but she remained mortal.

Checking to make sure the ice dragon's impaled foot still kept it trapped, Greeta turned her attention to the hot springs.

The ice dragon in the springs still slogged through the water toward Frayka, but the hot water had reduced it to the size of a mortal. Like Frayka, only its head remained above water.

"How dare you threaten us!" Frayka shouted at it. She glided slowly through the water, keeping just out of the ice dragon's reach. "We are Northlanders! We will fight you to the death!"

Greeta shuddered once more, this time filled with delight. She looked at her body, both relieved and disappointed to see she still had mortal form. She then hurried to the northern-most end of the springs and offered a hand to help Frayka haul herself out.

Keeping her eyes on the diminished dragon following her through the water, Frayka reached back, feeling for the rocky edge of the hot springs. Finding it, she moved quickly. She spun to face the edge and hoisted herself over it, ignoring Greeta.

Worried that the dragon in the hot springs would follow, Greeta checked its progress.

But the dragon's head merely bobbed in the water, making Greeta realize the hot springs had melted away everything else.

Finding her dagger, Frayka turned to face the final dragon.

The ice dragon stood upright again, screeching as it pulled its remaining foot up through the sword holding it to the ground. The creature paused to roar at the women, its frosty breath blowing their hair away from their faces. It then sprinted northward, its stump leaving divots behind in the grass.

"Come back here, you coward!" Frayka shouted, sprinting after it.

Greeta ran to her sword, still standing upright in the ground, and pulled it free. But when she turned to follow Frayka, she heard the young woman cry out and disappear into the ground.

CHAPTER 13

"Frayka!" Greeta cried, running toward her.

Remember to watch where you step!

Greeta slowed, mindful of the ground in front of every step she took. As an extra precaution, she poked at the grass with the point of her sword, feeling for weak places. Finally, she came to the place where Frayka had disappeared into the earth. Greeta discovered a narrow fissure, no wider than the length of her sword.

Peering into it, she discovered Frayka a short distance down, wedged between the narrowing walls of the fissure. She clung to the hilt of her dagger, which she had stabbed into the side of one wall.

"Are you all right?" Greeta said.

"Fine." Frayka glared up at her. "Get going! You can't let that dragon escape."

Looking at the horizon, Greeta shook her head. "It's already gone."

"That's no excuse. Run! Catch up with it!"

Greeta extended her arm down into the fissure. "I'm not leaving you behind. Give me your hand."

"No! Killing that dragon is crucial!"

The fissure shifted slightly, widening enough that Frayka would have fallen deeper had she not been bracing herself in place.

"This is no time to argue," Greeta said. "Take my hand."

The fissure shifted again, and Frayka obeyed, reaching up to wrap her hand around Greeta's forearm. Still bracing herself against each wall of the fissure, Frayka shimmied up with the help of her dagger and let Greeta haul her onto solid ground, the force of Greeta's pull sending them sprawling.

"You really have to watch where you step," Greeta said. She sat up and rubbed the dirt from her hands.

Sitting up next to her, Frayka shook her head in disgust. "It's too late. The ice dragon could have run anywhere, and there's no way to find it. I ought to punch you in the face."

Greeta recoiled at the sting of her words. "What?"

Dejected, Frayka wiped the blade of her dagger against the grass and then against her skirt. "You ruined the portents! This isn't how things were supposed to happen."

Thinking back, Greeta remembered someone saying something about Frayka and her portents but realized she had no idea what it meant. "I don't know what you're talking about."

Frayka tucked her dagger under her belt and glared at Greeta. "Of course you don't. Because you're not one of us! You're not a true Northlander!"

Those words made Greeta feel as if she'd gone back several weeks in time, back home in the Great Turtle Lands where the betrayal by her own sweetheart along with her cousin had convinced Greeta she belonged nowhere. That no one wanted her. That she had been rejected by

everyone she loved. She felt like an outcast among the Shining Star people and
now she felt like an outcast among the
Northlanders as well.

Don't let anyone tell you who you are.

Greeta recognized the ghostly voice of
Margreet whispering in her ear and took
those words to heart. She took a deep
breath to calm herself. She and Frayka
were on their own now, and it made more
sense to befriend than antagonize her. "I
belong here just as much as you."

Frayka snorted her disgust. "You don't
even understand the portents."

"Then explain it to me. What is the portents and why does it mean so much to
you?"

Sputtering in surprise, Frayka took a
few moments to compose herself. Eyeing
Greeta with caution, she said, "Sometimes
I see things that will happen in the future.
It's a gift passed down from my great-
grandmother. My father's grandmother."

Of course. Thorkel had talked about
how even though Frayka had mostly
Northlander blood, she looked like his
grandmother, a woman from the Far East.

"You see things? How?" Anxious to

learn more, Greeta wondered if Frayka's portents might be similar to walking in the Dreamtime.

Frayka became calmer. "Sometimes I have dreams that tell me the future. Other times I have waking dreams. I'll see what everyone else around me sees, but then I see the future on top of it. Months ago I saw what happened today. Before, the ice dragons have only watched us from a distance. In the portents, I saw them come to our settlement and shake the ground apart. I saw how I jumped over before it happened, how I stood on one side with the dragons and everyone else stood on the other side. It's why Father went to fetch you, so you people could make swords for us to fight the dragons." Frayka's voice quivered. "But what I didn't tell Father was that I saw myself fighting the dragons alone. I killed all of them. And that's how Njall became my husband." Fighting back tears, she said, "And now you've ruined everything!"

Greeta frowned. "But I heard Njall when the dragons came. He doesn't love you. He called you a freak."

"That was before." Collecting herself,

Frayka's tone turned cold. "When he saw me kill all the dragons, Njall saw he'd been wrong. That's when he fell in love with me."

Greeta remembered her own misjudgements of men. Her lifelong sweetheart had betrayed her. And when she'd met the Northlander Finehurst, Greeta thought she might love him until he proved himself to be a dangerous man. "A man who calls you a freak may not be the best man to marry."

Frayka rolled her eyes. "You think this is about love!"

"Of course. What else?"

Shaking her head, Frayka said, "You don't understand. People need someone who can read portents. It protects them from danger. It leads them to prosperity. It helps them survive."

Greeta understood. Her experience in the Dreamtime had probably meant the difference between her own life and death. "I understand."

"No, you don't," Frayka said. "It doesn't matter whether I love Njall or not. I don't even have to like him. What the portents told me is that he is the one man who can give me children who will also be able to read portents. With any other man, the gift of portents would die with me."

Greeta let Frayka's words sink in.

"If Njall fails to marry and have children with me," Frayka said, "the future of my people is at risk."

She's not like me. Not like me at all.

Frayka had lived all her life in this Northlander settlement with a mother and father, accepted by her people as a fellow Northlander even though she looked nothing like them. Greeta had lived her life without a mother, believing the Shining Star people accepted her as one of their own only to be betrayed. Greeta had grown up believing she'd already found a sweetheart who would spend his life with her, believing she'd be in love with him forever. And keenly aware of how much she needed that love, especially now that she'd lost it.

But Frayka didn't seem to have that need. She already had the love of a complete family as well as the respect of her people. And she cared about protecting them.

Of course. Why wouldn't you want to

keep the people who already love you safe?

Greeta had done the same thing weeks ago in the Great Turtle Lands when she thought Papa and Auntie Peppa were in danger of being discovered and controlled by Finehurst. She'd been willing to do anything to protect them.

Thinking about the next seven generations, Greeta decided she didn't know enough about Frayka's dilemma. "What will happen next? If that dragon gets away?"

Frayka heaved a sigh of defeat. "It goes back to the sorcerer that created the ice dragons and sent them to attack."

"Sorcerer?" Greeta said, startled by the revelation.

Frayka nodded. "The ice dragon will take information about us back to him. Then the sorcerer will know enough to send a more deadly threat next time. He'll succeed in destroying or enslaving us."

I can't take Frayka back to Blackstone. Not yet. How could I live with the possibility of her people facing tragedy when I can do something to prevent it right now?

The weight of her decision made Greeta feel weary, even though she believed with all her heart that it was the best decision to make. They had to stop the sorcerer's threat. That meant finding the ice dragon that had escaped. Once they killed it, Greeta could go back to the Northlander settlement with peace of mind.

But for now, Greeta felt as if she hadn't slept in weeks. Doing something as simple as taking a single step forward felt like an impossible task. She allowed herself the luxury of thinking about how much she wanted her old life back, even though she thought Wapiti had ruined it by betraying her. Greeta didn't care about the betrayal anymore. She longed for the simple joy of waking up in her own home and living the life she loved.

Greeta put those thoughts away. Running away to the life she'd left behind would make her a coward, indifferent to all but herself. That wasn't who Greeta wanted to be. For now, she had to focus on the task at hand. She would return home after all troubles in the Land of Ice were settled. "Maybe we can make things right."

Frayka shook her head. "I don't see how."

Greeta pointed at the divots left behind

by the ice dragon's stump of a leg. "We can follow it. And if we kill the last dragon, maybe that's all it will take to make things right again."

RESA NELSON

CHAPTER 14

"Fine," Frayka said, hauling herself to her feet. "I'll follow the dragon. You go back to Blackstone. See if you can find a way around the chasm."

Greeta stood beside her. "Maybe you didn't hear me. I said *we* can follow the last ice dragon. Both of us. Together."

"I don't need you to slow me down. Go home."

"No. We're the only ones separated from Blackstone. We're alone." Greeta thought back to her travels with Shadow, the shaman who taught her how to walk in the Dreamtime. She remembered how Shadow walked with one foot in the everyday world and the other in the Spirit world. And how

114

that led to Shadow living a life apart from other people. "But maybe we can be alone together."

Frayka snorted. "Nonsense. Leave me a-lone." She turned to take a step only to cry out in pain and stumble back to the ground. Startled, she lifted her skirts to expose her feet. One of her ankles had swollen.

Greeta dropped to her knees, examining the swollen ankle. "You're injured. You can't travel alone. You shouldn't walk on this foot."

"It's a simple twist. I'm fine." Frayka stood and hobbled a few steps. "There's nothing wrong with me."

But the next step made Frayka cry out and fall again.

Greeta had seen several injuries like this in her own village, ranging from children who stumbled in play to men who limped back from a victorious hunt. She'd seen the healer in her village help many people with such an injury. And Greeta realized she had exactly what she needed at hand to help Frayka.

"You're drenched," Greeta said. "And hurt. You should take off your clothes and let them dry in the sun, or you'll get sick. I can treat your ankle. By the time your clothes dry, it might be easier to walk on it."

"But the ice dragon—"

"We can still follow it. The tracks will still be there a few hours from now."

Frayka shook her head. Her face twisted in pain when she climbed back to her feet and hobbled a few more steps in pursuit of the dragon.

Greeta said, "If you let your clothes dry and give your foot some rest, I'll let you use my sword to walk. You can use it like a cane. Or maybe we can strap it to your leg to help you walk."

Ignoring her, Frayka took another step, only to grunt in pain when her leg buckled beneath her. Reluctantly, she said, "Alright. But when my ankle is strong enough for me to walk on my own, you must go back to Blackstone. I won't allow you to stay with me any longer than necessary."

Absolutely not. But you don't need to know that yet.

"Agreed," Greeta said.

After helping Frayka hobble back to the hot springs, Greeta took the woman's drenched clothing and laid each piece flat on the grass to dry in the sun. She then found the remnants of the dragon's foot and used a rock to crush the ice into small shards. Telling Frayka to sit on the grass, Greeta then piled the ice shards on top of and all around the woman's swollen ankle.

Frayka shivered. "It's too cold."

"It's perfect. Back home, the healers use snow, but they say ice is better when you can find it." Greeta paused, surveying the hot springs and the grounds surrounding it.

Frayka squinted at her. "There's no more ice."

"I'm looking for something else. The healers also use plants." Greeta stopped herself, realizing she'd nearly mentioned Wapiti's name because his uncle had a knack with plants and healing. She'd once heard him say that all plant life must be treated with the same respect given to all animals. The uncle had said all life, no matter what form, were brothers and sisters to mortals.

"The plants here are useless," Frayka said with a dismissive wave of her hand. "They're nothing like the plants in the

Northlands. They have no value."

"All life has value," Greeta said. She walked past Frayka to a stretch of vegetation growing a short distance from the hot springs.

She knelt to get a closer look. Soft green moss dotted black rocks peeking through the vegetation. Some plants looked like tall, spiky grass, while others had large, broad leaves. A vine-like plant with purple leaves ran through the rest of the vegetation like a river.

Greeta closed her eyes, thinking back to every time someone in her village had been injured and treated, trying to remember what plant had been used and what it looked like. She thought about Wapiti's uncle and the stories he had told. She remembered how he said plants spoke to him, not with words but in the way they reacted to his words and touch.

"Which one of you can help her?" Greeta said softly. Reaching out with one hand, she trailed her fingertips across each different type of plant, letting her touch linger upon their leaves.

Nothing.

A new thought struck her. Wapiti's uncle had talked about how plants well known to the Shining Star people were like old friends that never hesitated to greet them.

And how plants unknown to the Shining Star people must be treated with the same courtesy and respect anyone would give to a stranger entering one's village.

Greeta said, "Please. She needs healing, and I don't know what to do for her. I would so very greatly appreciate any guidance you can give me." This time, she held her hand above each plant. Perhaps touching them had been an inappropriate act of familiarity.

The wind kicked up, and a broad leaf lifted to touch her palm.

Greeta caught her breath. Had the wind merely blown the leaf upward? Or had it risen on its own accord?

"What's taking so long?" Frayka shouted.

The broad leaf shuddered and lowered itself.

"Please don't be put off by her," Greeta whispered. She knelt in front of the plant, bringing herself to its level. "Frayka is passionate about helping her people. I think that's a good and noble thing, don't you?"

With the tentative nature of a shy child, the broad leaf pressed itself into her hand.

"Thank you," Greeta whispered. "May I take several of you?"

Several other broad leaves extended toward her. One purple-leaf vine snaked around them.

Of course! Something needs to tie them around Frayka's ankle.

"Many thanks," Greeta said, picking several broad leaves as well as the vine.

Once the ice surrounding Frayka's ankle melted, Greeta wrapped it with the broad leaves.

Frayka grunted. "They sting."

"Good. That means they're already helping you heal." Greeta wrapped the vine around the leaves several times and then tied it to hold them in place.

Frayka stood and placed her weight on the ankle. Her face twisted in agony.

Greeta thought about all that had happened since last night. Along Papa's side, she'd worked in the smithery through the night. The dragons had attacked in the very early hours of the morning. Greeta had then fought ice dragons, hauled Frayka out of the fissure, and tended to her twisted ankle. Greeta felt exhausted and suspected that Frayka hadn't slept much before the dragons attacked. "We should try to sleep. Rest will help you heal."

"No," Frayka said, taking a pained step. "Father says strange things have happened ever since our people arrived. Things that would drive most people away in fear. Until I face the sorcerer, he will keep making horrible creatures to terrorize us."

"Have the ice dragons attacked for a long time?"

Frayka shook her head. "Only for the past year. But there have been other things."

Greeta's curiosity made her want to ask what those other things were, but being cut off from Papa, Auntie Peppa, Thorkel, Rognvald, and the rest of the Northlander settlement made her feel vulnerable enough. She didn't need anything else to make her feel even more uneasy.

"We think the ice dragons might be the sorcerer's scouts. That they take information back to him that could help him destroy us." Frayka's lips became a grim line of determination. "It's too late to keep that dragon from reaching the sorcerer. But if we can follow its tracks, they may lead us to him."

"The tracks aren't going anywhere. We can take a night to rest and heal." Greeta swallowed hard. "But what happens if we find the sorcerer?"

Accepting Greeta's idea, Frayka sank to the ground and eased her leafy ankle to rest. "When we find the sorcerer," she said, "we kill him."

CHAPTER 15

When she fell asleep, Greeta dreamed.

In her dreams, Greeta found herself walking beside Shadow, the shaman who taught her how to walk in the Dreamtime. In the bright light of morning, they strolled on an empty beach. Greeta felt the warmth of the sand through the soles of her simple leather shoes. The waves crashed so loudly that they had to shout to be heard above them.

"I like dragons," Shadow said. "I like all animals because they are our brothers and sisters, but dragons are so different and exciting. I like their fearlessness. And the way they whip their tails around. And all those teeth!"

Greeta smiled. Shadow talked a lot, but that made sense to Greeta. Even though she'd spent little time with the shaman, it seemed Shadow spent most of her time alone. No wonder she liked to talk whenever someone showed up who could listen.

"You turned into a dragon." Shadow smiled at her. "I wish I could have been there to see it. I'm not a shapeshifter myself, but I've met some. I like shapeshifters just as much as I like animals."

Greeta felt her heart quicken. "But I don't know how I did it! Why did I change into a dragon? Why had it never happened before? What if I need to do it again?"

Shadow shrugged. "I'm a shaman, not a shapeshifter."

"But I need answers."

A rogue wave crept upon the shore, taking Shadow in its grasp and ripping her out to sea. Inexplicably, it left Greeta behind. "Shadow!"

The shaman laughed, riding the waves. "Farewell, Greeta! I'll see you on the other side of the great sea!" Within moments, the ocean swept Shadow so far out to the horizon that Greeta could no longer see her.

Stepping toward the water, Greeta cried out when something sharp stabbed the sole of her foot. She halted and poked at the sand with her toes until a small red stone emerged. She picked up the stone and held it up to the light. It sparkled like a gemstone.

The sun plummeted from the sky like a dead bird and fell below the horizon. Moments later, the moon took a more leisurely journey. But as it climbed in the black night sky, its color changed like iron cooling after being pulled from the fire: from yellow to orange to a dull blood red.

Greeta trembled, not understanding why the world was changing so quickly and in such a strange way. She held onto the stone, wrapping her fist around it, squeezing her anxiety into it.

Stars swarmed the sky, brightening until Greeta had to shield her eyes from them.

Open your hand.

Recognizing the voice of Margreet's ghost, Greeta obeyed. The red stone had turned black. It became a stone of darkness.

The light from the blinding stars fell into the stone, forcing the blackness out of it until it looked like Greeta held a tiny star in her hand.

Margreet whispered in Greeta's ear again.

Remember this: Your mother tried to help me. She stood by my side. She taught me to fight, just as I taught you. She did not fail me. I failed her by not listening closely enough.

Never make my mistake.

The stone of light cast a brilliant beam toward the sea and across its waters. In the far, far distance, it illuminated an island that looked like a shard of ice.

The Land of Ice.

Be true to your path, Greeta. Never doubt it.

Bright white light spilled out of the stone, embedding itself in Greeta's hand. She cried out from the fiery heat and tried to drop the stone, but it wouldn't fall from her hand. She tried pushing it out of her hand, but the stone clung to it with sharp edges, digging until it drew blood.

Embrace your destiny, for it is yours and yours alone.

When Greeta saw her hand burst into

starlight, she screamed.

"Greeta!" Frayka said.

Blinking fast and hard, Greeta stared at her surroundings. No longer in the Great Turtle Lands from her dreams, she stood next to the hot springs where the ice dragon had melted. The gentle light of morning had grown stronger, and the sun had reached its highest peak. Panic-stricken, Greeta looked at her hands, solid and fine. Feeling her heart pound, she rubbed her hands together to make sure.

She saw no stone of any color.

Frayka stood next to her, her black eyes piercing and concerned. "You walk in your sleep all the time?"

Realizing she was standing, Greeta wondered if she had acted out her dream without knowing it. "No. Not until now."

"Good. Don't do it again." Frayka walked a few steps, showing only a slight limp. "Looks like your healers back home know what they're doing. The twist got better fast."

Greeta looked at the sun to make sure it stayed put in the sky. "I'm glad I remembered." She almost said the plants helped her recognize them, but she didn't think

Frayka would be happy to hear it. Instead, she looked around until she found the unfinished sword and picked it up. "Do you want to use this to lean on when you walk?" She braced herself, expecting Frayka to tell her to go back to Blackstone.

Frayka shook her head. "Keep it." She pointed at a divot in the ground left when the last ice dragon had run away on one good foot and one stump that sank into the ground with every stride. "Let's go."

Greeta stared at her in surprise until she saw how Frayka limped.

Frayka has healed enough to walk, but she still struggles. That's why she's letting me stay with her.

Greeta heaved a quiet sigh of relief, happy she didn't have to argue with Frayka.

The women followed the trail of divots all day, resting every so often to drink from the skin Frayka had slung over her shoulder and eat from the small pouch of seeds and nuts she had tied to her belt in anticipation of her own portents.

The countryside spread wide and flat before them. The trail ran through grassy fields, but they encountered occasional stretches of black rocky terrain running alongside or through the fields like frozen rivers so ancient they had solidified forever. After Frayka's slip into the hidden fissure, they both moved with caution while keeping a good pace.

By the time the sun dipped back down to graze the horizon, they trudged up a sloping hill next to a cliff that looked as if it had just been pushed up through the earth, grass and vines hanging over its edge. When they neared the top of the hill, the sound of rushing water filled the air.

Reaching the top, Greeta and Frayka looked down at several flat expansive stones, each the size of the settlement they had left behind. The stones stood like steps, each slightly lower than the next. Water emerged from a cave at the base of the cliff and spilled steadily over the highest stone, cascading down the others until the fall formed a river running east toward the sea.

"Look!" Frayka shouted above the roar of the waterfall. She pointed at the trail of divots left by the ice dragon, which ended at the edge of the flat stones.

Greeta considered the breadth of the

unusual waterfall blocking their path. The cliff and cave opening stood to their left, making it impossible to head north. The waterfall spread before them, and the river prevented them from going east. The only other option meant heading south, back toward where they had started.

Gesturing for Frayka to follow, Greeta picked her way through a band of small rocks to the edge of the highest flat stone. She knelt and reached forward to touch the water. Standing and turning back toward Frayka, she shouted, "It's cold!"

Frayka shrugged.

Greeta pointed at the cave. "This water comes from underground, where it's cold and dark. It's frigid. The ice dragon could have walked across this part of the waterfall without melting." She reconsidered. "Much."

"If it crossed," Frayka said, "then its trail continues on the other side."

"I think so."

"Then we follow." Frayka hitched up her skirts, revealing her ankle still wrapped in leaves and vines.

"Wait!" Greeta tucked the unfinished sword high under her arm. Everyone knew how quickly water would damage iron. "The stone will be slick. Let me help you walk." Stepping into the rushing water, Greeta found it came up to her knees. The stone felt smooth and polished beneath her feet. She gripped the tang of the sword and extended it toward Frayka, knowing its unfinished edges and point posed no harm to her. "Here!"

Frayka shifted her grip on her skirts to one hand and then wrapped her free fingers around the blade of the sword.

"Be careful," Greeta said. "It's slick."

Nodding her understanding, Frayka stepped into the water, and the women shuffled gingerly across the slippery, expansive stone. Greeta took her time leading the way, careful to find a foothold that seemed stable before completing each step. Spray from the water crashing onto the next flat stone below filled the air, and the bright light of day created rainbow colors in the mist. By the time the women walked halfway across, Greeta's legs had gone numb from the icy temperature of the water.

A roar rumbled from the mouth of the cave, making the smooth stone tremble beneath their feet.

Greeta and Frayka looked toward the cave to see the water at its mouth rise and take the shape of a woman. It opened its jaws and roared again. The woman made of water spread her arms and shook them until the water rushing past Greeta and Frayka churned into whirlpools.

"Keep moving!" Frayka shouted at Greeta, still holding onto the sword's blade. "We can make it."

The power of the whirlpools, now rising steadily around each woman, kept Greeta in her place until she shoved her way through and dragged Frayka with her.

The woman made of water roared again, and cool air blasted from her mouth. Instead of eyes, her face had two open sockets. Ribbons of water whipped like long, free-flowing hair around her head.

A whirlpool wrapped itself around Greeta like a cocoon, wrenching the sword away from her. All she could see and hear and taste was the ice-like water, and it squeezed her like a giant's hand, making her gasp for breath.

Greeta felt herself lifted and thrown downward. The force sent her tumbling down the long steps of the waterfall, spinning and dizzy, kicking and thrashing to break free until her head hit a hard surface and she felt herself slip away into nothingness.

CHAPTER 16

Greeta struggled to come awake when she felt icy talons grip her feet, a grip that pulled and tugged, seeming to gobble her up.

It's an ice dragon trying to kill me! It must have been lying in wait!

She tried to jump to her feet only to discover she'd been swept all the way down the waterfall and into the river below. Greeta thrashed in the water, sputtering every time the water entered her mouth. Her soaked clothing weighed her down like iron, trying to drag her to the bottom of the river. The rushing water filled her ears, blocking out all other sound, and poured across her face, blinding her.

The talons dug tighter into her skin and pulled Greeta through the hurried river and onto the bank.

Frantic, Greeta reached for the unfinished sword only to realize she couldn't find it. She spun, looking for the ice dragon. Instead, she saw Frayka.

"By the gods!" Frayka said. "You weigh more than a hundred buckets of water." She sank to sit on the grass, rearranged her own drenched clothing, and stretched out her legs.

Sinking next to her, Greeta was glad to see the plants still wrapped around Frayka's ankle, even though they seemed to shiver and shake off droplets of water. "Thank you."

Frayka raised her eyebrows, looking genuinely surprised. "For what?"

Greeta pointed at the river. "I would have drowned if you hadn't pulled me out. You saved my life."

Frayka sputtered a laugh. "I doubt it. You would have floated for awhile and then come awake. I figured it's easier for you to get back to Blackstone from here than wake up in some place you don't know and have to figure it out."

Leaning to one side, Greeta shook the water out of her ear, thinking she must have misheard. "What?"

Frayka pointed downstream. "There's a narrow part with plenty of boulders in the river. You can use them to step across to the other side. All you have to do is backtrack."

"And what will you be doing?"

"What the portents intend me to do." Frayka pointed at her ankle. "I assumed this ankle was still too weak. I was wrong. Made it through all that nonsense the water witch threw at us, and I feel better than ever."

Greeta's head spun from too much happening too fast. "The water witch?"

"Don't tell me you didn't see her." Frayka snorted. "It must be that sorcerer with the ice dragons who put her there." Frayka turned and shouted at the waterfall towering behind them. "But your plan didn't work! I defeated you!"

"*We* defeated her," Greeta said, correcting her.

"Of course. The water witch threw you down the waterfall and you passed out. Thank you for your help in defeating her."

Frayka's words stung, but Greeta realized she spoke the truth.

"And by the way," Frayka added. "I saved your sword. I'm keeping it. A girl can never have too many weapons." She pushed her hands at Greeta. "Now shoo. Be along your way. Give my best to Father."

"We agreed I will leave when you've healed," Greeta said.

"I'm fine now." Frayka stood, although her wet clothes weighed down every motion, making her look slow and awkward. However, she did seem better if not completely healed. "I don't need you."

"If you walk in wet clothes, you'll catch cold. Maybe even worse." Having caught her breath, Greeta climbed to her feet. "The sun is strong. It won't take long for our clothes to dry if we lay them out."

Frayka ignored her. She picked up the unfinished sword from the grass and trudged away.

Frayka is still at risk, which means the next seven generations are still at risk. I can't leave her yet.

Grateful that Papa had told her to wear men's clothing for blacksmithing, Greeta found them more difficult to move in when wet but could see her mobility came easier than Frayka's in her long, heavily drenched skirts. Greeta ran and caught up with Frayka, walking by her side. "What if the purpose of your portents was to bring me here? Thorkel and Rognvald sailed to the Great Turtle Lands because you told them about your portents. They knew my mother. And they knew about me."

Staring straight ahead, Frayka said, "I don't care. Go away."

Greeta steeled herself, daring to reveal the secret about herself she'd discovered mere weeks ago. "I think they brought me here because I can turn into a dragon."

Frayka stopped and stared at Greeta. "Don't tell me you actually believe that nonsense my father has been talking about you."

Her words startled Greeta. "You don't believe him?"

Frayka pressed her lips together. "No one believes it except Father and Rognvald." Her face took a pained expression. "Oh, those awful stories about the old days in the Northlands! They say you were a dragon just hatched, but who's to say they weren't imagining things? The Northlands and Midlands and Southlands were falling apart. People were scared. They weren't thinking right, and who's to say they haven't exaggerated what they remember?"

Greeta crossed her arms, and irritation tugged down the corners of her mouth. "When everyone remembers the same thing, it's a safe bet they remember the truth. I *can* turn into a dragon. People back home say I'm a shapeshifter. I turned into a dragon just a few weeks ago."

Frayka smirked. "Fine. Turn into a dragon now then."

"I don't know how to control it." The tinge of shame in her own voice surprised Greeta. "When I turned into a dragon, it just happened. I haven't figured out why yet."

Frayka's words were clear and plain. "Go home." She hiked up her heavy, wet skirts and forged ahead across a steep embankment.

Greeta refused to give up. Catching up and matching Frayka's steps stride for stride, she said, "What if I'm supposed to help you?"

Frayka laughed. "By turning into a dragon when you least expect it?"

"Maybe." Greeta set her jaw, determined not to be dissuaded. "Or maybe we can accomplish more by working together than working apart."

Nearing the top of the embankment, Greeta ran ahead, hoping to see something in their path ahead that would prove her point. The sight spreading out before her made Greeta catch her breath, and she took it all in while waiting for Frayka to catch up.

The trail of divots left by the ice dragon continued on the other side of the embankment, a sloping hill leading to a wide lake below, surrounded by forest. A low range of uneven and grassy hills blocked most of the view behind the forest.

But in the far, far distance Greeta saw a mountain of rock and dirt. On its peak stood a castle of ice, gleaming in the sunlight.

"Do you think that's where the ice dragons came from?" Greeta said.

Nodding, Frayka said, "I think it's where we'll find the sorcerer that made them."

When they continued, they kept the distant ice castle directly in sight.

CHAPTER 17

Because Frayka refused to stop to let their clothing dry in the sun, Greeta walked naked and barefoot. She tied the arms of her shirt around her waist while holding the waist of her pants above her head, letting the wind blow through the legs. Once her pants were dry she put them on and repeated the process with the shirt. Testing to make sure it was no longer damp, Greeta slipped the shirt over her head, still walking barefoot with her shoes in hand. Keeping by Frayka's side, she approached the lake they'd seen from the top of the crest by the waterfall. "You have to let your clothes dry or you'll catch your death."

Ignoring her, Frayka kept walking. She halted and pointed at a thicket of trees with no foliage that surrounded the lake. "I've heard of those. They're skeleton trees."

Greeta stared at the trees standing barely taller than a mortal, branches reaching high, wood pale and dry. "You mean they're dead?"

"Not dead. They don't grow any kind of leaves. They're like skeletons." Frayka lowered her voice as if not wanting to be overheard. "And they're said to be wicked gossips, so mind what you say within their earshot."

Greeta hesitated. She knew plants like flowers and vines could hear but had always assumed trees were deaf to mortal speech because she'd never heard of anyone having much luck talking to them. "Trees don't have ears!"

"They listen nonetheless."

Greeta sobered when she saw Frayka was serious, watching her companion as they approached the trees.

Frayka pointed at the trail of divots running between the trees but said nothing. She gestured for Greeta to follow while leading the way through the skeleton trees, ducking under their limbs.

A rushing sound surrounded Greeta, and she assumed it had to be the wind until she realized the air stood still. Listening more closely, she heard faint whispers cascading from tree to tree.

These are Northlanders.

But Northlanders are pale. Look at that dark one!

Northlanders stand the tallest of all mortals. The dark one is as tall as the pale one. They both have Northlander blood.

Quick! Spread the word!

The whispers rushed to the right and the left like rippling waves, and the trees trembled as they passed their gossip.

Nudging Greeta, Frayka pointed at the trail of divots leading straight into the wide, large lake.

Without thinking, Greeta protested, "We can't go through the lake. Your clothes are still wet. You're sure to get sick."

The trees next to them shuddered with delight.

They plan to cross the lake!

They're giving chase. Following the path.

But the dark one is ill. Weak and help-

less. Easy to attack and defeat.

Tell while there's still time!

Frayka clamped her hand over Greeta's mouth and glared at her. Speaking up, plain and clear, she said, "I'm fine. I feel perfectly well."

The dark one lies.

She doesn't want us to know.

She lies, she lies, she lies.

Spread the word!

Heading toward the water's edge, Frayka picked up the hem of her skirts, raising them above her knees by tucking the hem under her belt. She withdrew her dagger and held it high above her head along with the unfinished sword.

Greeta stripped, holding her clothing above her head while she followed Frayka into the lake. The water's bitterly cold temperature shocked her into stillness for a few seconds. Prepared to swim, Greeta decided to wait until the water came above her waist so she wouldn't kick the lake bottom with every stroke. But the water merely lapped around her hips, never rising higher. She slogged through the lake with more ease than Frayka, held back by the skirts around her thighs.

Joining Frayka's side once more, Greeta said, "What kind of lake is this? Can it be this shallow all the way across?"

"It must be. Why else would an ice dragon risk coming into it? Ice floats. In a deep lake, the creature's legs couldn't move against the bottom of the lake. It wouldn't have a way to propel itself."

"Ice dragons can't swim?"

"It seems to me they'd melt faster that way."

Greeta wasn't so sure she agreed but kept quiet. She didn't want to argue. She still worried about Frayka's health, knowing they both needed to be at their best for whatever they'd soon be facing.

They spent the entire afternoon crossing the shallow lake, its shores buzzing with the talk of the skeleton trees. By the time they reached the other shore, Greeta struggled, so exhausted that she could hardly move one foot in front of the other.

Frayka held one finger against her lips, gesturing for Greeta to stay silent.

Greeta obeyed and resisted the urge not only to talk but to collapse on solid ground the moment she felt it underfoot.

The Northlanders are out of the lake!

Spread the word, spread the word!
Tell all who should know!

Not liking the sound of what the trees whispered, Greeta gave Frayka a questioning look.

But Frayka walked through the trees toward the rocky field beyond them, leaving a trail of water behind as it dripped from her clothes.

Greeta followed, happy when they reached the open field where her skin soon would dry in the sun, even though it had fallen low in the sky. Within minutes she redressed in the clothing she'd kept dry by holding it above her head all afternoon. Relief washed through her aching arms when she finally let them rest by her side.

Frayka paused, studying the rocky ground. Moments later, she pointed at a single divot between stones.

Greeta followed while Frayka searched for each tell-tale step left behind by the ice dragon, creeping slowly across the field to trace them.

When they reached a plateau of stone, Frayka studied the stone and the dirt surrounding it. Glancing back at the lake and the distance between them and the gossiping trees, she turned to Greeta and said, "It ends here. The dragon must have crossed this plateau, but then it could have gone anywhere." She swept an arm across the enormous plateau, stretching from horizon to horizon.

Greeta studied the plateau, stretching not only wide but deep. She pointed across it, straight ahead. "That looks like an edge. If there's ground on the other side, maybe the trail will pick up again. Maybe the ice dragon kept going in the same direction and simply crossed it."

"It's going to the ice castle we saw," Frayka said. "That's the only thing that makes sense. All I have to do is go to the ice castle." When they crossed the plateau, she shivered.

Greeta bit her tongue, worried but tired of trying to advise Frayka about her health.

The solid stone, warm from the sun, felt good under Greeta's bare feet. When they reached the edge, a field lay beneath the edge of the plateau. To the right and not far away stood a group of towering columns made of the same black rock Greeta had seen near Blackstone.

Frayka sneezed and shuddered.

Greeta pointed first at the ground and then to the left. "Look. I see the trail again."

Frayka sneezed again.

"You're not well." Greeta knew Frayka was no child. Frayka was her own woman and responsible for making her own decisions. But when people became ill, it often impaired their judgment. "You can't go on in your condition."

Surprisingly, Frayka hesitated. "It might be a good idea to get some rest."

Seizing the opportunity, Greeta pointed at the towering black columns. "That place looks like it could protect us. We could build a fire. Get you warm and dry."

Nodding her consent, Frayka allowed Greeta to lead her down to the field beyond the plateau and onto a path of black sand that led them into a maze created by dozens of high black columns, each one shaped differently by time and wind. Although the towers had appeared solid from the distance, up close the surface of each structure looked as lacy as leaves partially eaten by insects.

Wandering deeper into the complex of towers, Greeta worried first that they seemed to be getting lost among them and second that Frayka had become silent and couldn't seem to stop shivering. But then she noticed a warm yellow glow emerging through the lacy walls of one tower and at the same time heard singing.

Singing meant people must be nearby. And the warm yellow glow could mean a fire.

Taking Frayka by the hand, Greeta dragged her around the column until she discovered what seemed to be an entrance. Following the yellow light and the sound of men's melodious voices, the women soon found themselves stepping into a dark and cavernous hall where dozens of men sat on roughly hewn benches surrounding the largest hearth fire Greeta had ever seen. The men appeared like black shadows against the light of the flames.

One man stood, pointing at them. "There they are!"

The other men stopped singing, turning to look at Greeta and Frayka.

"Come join us, Northlanders," the man

shouted. "The trees told us to expect you."

Greeta heaved a sigh of relief at the sound of friendly voices. But when Frayka spoke, the edge in her voice gave Greeta a chill.

"Who are you?" Frayka shouted, standing firm. "Are you native to this land?"

The men laughed. The standing one said, "No more than you. Most of us, Northlanders like you. Others, Midlanders. Others from the western islands. We even have a Southlander or two."

The aroma of a rich, hearty stew thick with spices filled the air. Greeta took a step toward the men, but Frayka clamped a warning hand on her shoulder.

"They're like us," Greeta whispered. "We can rest here."

"I see no other women," Frayka whispered. "Never trust men when there are no women to keep them in line." She handed the unfinished sword to Greeta and withdrew her own dagger, making no attempt to hide their weapons.

"Sister Northlander," the standing man said with disappointment. "Think of us as your kin. We all have wives and daughters. We'd no more harm you than we would our own girls."

Greeta's empty stomach twisted so hard it made her wince in pain. "We need to eat," she whispered to Frayka. "We're losing strength."

"Keep your guard up," Frayka murmured. "And be ready to run if need be."

The women kept their weapons in hand as they approached the fire, while the standing man scooped stew out of the cauldron hanging over the fire and into two wooden bowls, holding them out.

Overwhelmed by hunger, Greeta tucked the sword under her arm and accepted the bowl, holding the rim up to her lips to eat directly from it. She didn't realize Frayka hadn't done the same until Greeta had devoured the contents of the entire bowl.

Frayka stood a few steps behind Greeta, pointing her dagger at the men, ready to fight. "What are you?"

Startled by Frayka's question, Greeta took a closer look at the shadowy figures surrounding the fire. Her eyes had adjusted to the dim light, and for the first time she sensed something strange about them. Although shaped like mortals, there was a peculiar roughness to their silhouettes. And spots of fire flickered where their eyes should have been.

Greeta looked down at the empty bowl, wondering if she'd made a mistake.

"Not to worry," the standing man said, stepping forward and taking the empty bowl from her. "The food we gave you is good. There's no harm in it."

Now Greeta understood. The standing man didn't appear to be made of flesh and bone. Instead, he seemed to be made of small chunks of black rocks and bits of driftwood. Tiny vines with red berries covered his head like hair. Similar to the ice dragons, nothing seemed to bind all his parts together. Instead, they fit together like a puzzle, allowing him the same range of motion as a mortal although a bit stilted.

He offered the other bowl of stew to Frayka, who still stood several paces behind Greeta. "Eat up," he said to Frayka. "We like our mortals nice and plump before we put them in the cooking pot."

CHAPTER 18

Terrified, Greeta said, "You told us you'd no more harm us than your own kin!"

"If any of our kin still lived," the standing man said, "we would not harm them."

Frayka straightened her spine. "I know you! You're Erik, Ethelred's son."

Whispering to Greeta, Frayka said, "They're not monsters or sorcerers! No need to fear. They're just men." After a moment's pause, she added, "Although they're no longer in mortal form."

Frayka pointed at Erik's hair of vines and red berries. "I heard you're one of the few red-headed Northlanders."

"That's not real hair," Greeta whispered.

Frayka ignored her and continued. "My father told me stories about how you believed there had to be other lands on the other side of the sea. You're the one who found the Land of Vines!"

The standing man, Erik, handed the bowl of stew rejected by Frayka to one of his companions. "In my day, that's true." His voice took an edge. "But my day is gone." He gestured toward the dozens of other strange men surrounding him. "All our days are gone!"

Greeta's fear fell away, replaced by curiosity. Frayka knew of these men and looked comfortable with them. If Frayka had heard stories about Erik, then he must have been a true mortal not very long ago. So how could he have become such a strange creature? "What happened to you?"

Erik's eyes flamed brighter. "Now is not the time to try my patience."

"She doesn't know what happened in the Northlands," Frayka said, taking a step forward. Her tone now sounded confident, and Frayka moved with ease. "She was born in the Northlands, but she doesn't remember it. She's from the Land of Vines."

Erik's eyes flickered until streams of smoke rolled out of them. "Impossible!"

The other men grumbled in agreement.

"It's true," Greeta said, perplexed. "Why should it be impossible? My father and auntie took me across the sea in a Northlander ship, and we settled in a village of Shining Star people."

"Liar!" another man yelled, pointing an accusing finger at her. "Everyone knows the Vinelanders are deadly warriors."

"Horrible, screeching demons," another man shouted.

Erik crossed his rocky arms, and a few pebbles came loose and fell to the ground. "Had you met any Vinelanders, they would have slaughtered you on sight."

"But that isn't what happened," Greeta said. "I don't remember our landing, but I know we could have been killed. There is a reason why it didn't happen." She paused, hoping that telling the truth would be the right decision. "I'm the reason."

Erik and all the other strange men laughed, the light from the fire flickering against the walls surrounding them.

"I can tell the story I've been told," Greeta said, daring to take a step closer to the men sitting around the enormous hearth fire. Papa and Auntie Peppa had told her many stories about Northlanders, and she remembered that Northlanders were easily transfixed by fantastic tales. Luckily, all Greeta had to do was tell the truth. "It began when our ship encountered a terrible storm at sea."

"When they set sail from here to the Land of Vines," Frayka added, her voice dark and menacing.

The strange men responded by settling down and turning their full attention to the women.

Realizing they responded to the way Frayka spoke, Greeta made her voice just as dark and menacing. "They say the storm was so violent that it ripped the ship apart!"

Some of the men gasped, while others leaned forward, their fire-like eyes subdued into glowing embers.

"But the ship had travelled close enough to shore that the storm hurled us onto land. My Papa climbed out of the sea and onto the beach, but he couldn't find me."

"You were a mere babe," Erik murmured.

"No," Greeta said. "Because I was a dragon not long hatched out of my shell."

One of the men laughed. Although he spoke Northlander, his accent sounded peculiar. "Impossible."

"Not impossible," Erik said, keeping his gaze fixed on Greeta. "Not if she's a shapeshifter."

The man with the strange accent laughed again. "Rubbish! Everyone knows there is no such thing. Only stories we tell our children."

Erik turned and pointed at him. "Only in your Southlands. Shapeshifters are real in the Northlands." Erik paused and corrected himself. "*Were* real. Said to be plentiful in the old days and mostly died out. But we had some left."

The strange men then broke out arguing, their voices so loud and strained that Greeta could understand little of what they shouted at each other. Finally, Erik yelled at them all until they settled down. Once they'd become quiet, he said, "Let the little girl finish her story."

Greeta thought about how to frame the

story so they'd understand it more easily. "A Vinelander had read a portent that strangers would come to attack his people. He hid and watched us, and he planned to kill us. He saw some debris on the beach: the dragon masthead of our ship and a pile of dead skin."

"Dead skin?" Frayka said, now as engrossed as the strange men in Greeta's story.

Of course. She's hearing it for the first time. We haven't told anyone in Blackstone. It was only when we sailed here that Auntie Peppa told me this part of the story for the first time, and then it was in secret.

Greeta nodded. "The Vinelander saw a dragon tail thrashing. He later said it was larger than any lizard he'd ever seen and knew it had to be a dragon. And then he saw me. That's when he knew I was a shapeshifter. In mortal form, I had become a toddler. I stepped out of the dead dragon skin I had shed and called for my Papa. The Vinelander stayed hidden, wanting to see how many of us there were."

Erik piped up. "They're tricky. He'd want to figure out if he could kill you himself or needed help to do it."

"I believe so." Greeta nodded again. "He watched me find my Papa, and then we found my Auntie Peppa. I must have seen the Vinelander hidden in the grass, because I went running to him."

This part of the story Greeta knew very well. Only since learning Uncle Killing Crow had seen her change from a dragon into a little girl did she realize the poignancy of what happened next. "I must have assumed the Vinelander was my family, too, because I acted just as excited to see him as my kin." Greeta chewed her lower lip, keenly aware of how much she missed the land she knew as home and all the people she loved and had left behind. She fought her longing to go back to the everyday life she loved. It would have to wait for now.

All became so quiet and still that Greeta could hear only the crackle of the hearth fire. "When the Vinelander tells the story, he says I made his heart melt. The next thing that happened was he looked into my Auntie Peppa's eyes and knew she was the love of his life. The woman he'd been waiting to meet." Greeta took a deep breath. "The Vinelander who meant to kill us is my Uncle Killing Crow."

The men gasped in disbelief.

Erik crossed his arms. "Liar."

Frayka strolled over to the hearth fire and leaned toward the simmering cauldron of stew. The discomfort she previously exhibited toward the dead men had vanished.

Greeta noticed the corners of Frayka's mouth turn up slightly.

Frayka looks like she's the one in charge. I have a feeling she wants to toy with them.

Frayka stabbed the contents with her dagger and impaled a chunk of potato, blowing on it to make it cool faster. "It's no lie," Frayka said. "My own father retrieved this girl and her family from the Vinelanders. He says they all lived together like kin. The Vinelanders treated these people with our own Northlander blood like their own." She bit into the potato chunk and pulled it from the dagger into her mouth.

The men argued the merits of Frayka's claim, while Erik took a step closer to Greeta, looking her up and down with the fire in his eye sockets. "Prove you're a dragon. Change into one now."

"Don't bother asking," Frayka piped up. "She can't do it on command." She smacked one of the strange men sitting by the hearth with the back of her hand, gestureing for him to move over. When he made room for her on the bench, she plopped down between him and the man with the funny Southlander accent.

"What do you mean?" the Southlander said. "She's either a shapeshifter or she's not." Facing Greeta, he said, "Which one are you?"

"I'm a shapeshifter," Greeta said. "I can turn into a dragon. But there's been no one to teach me how. It just happened, and I can't figure out how to do it again."

When Erik drummed his rocky fingers against his crossed arms, one of his fingers fell off. Oblivious to its absence, he said, "What were the circumstances? Where were you when you changed into a dragon?"

Greeta launched into the story from the beginning, telling them how her lifelong sweetheart, Wapiti, had ridiculed Greeta behind her back and taken up with her married cousin. She told them how the shaman Shadow had arrived at the Shining Star village where she lived and offered to teach Greeta to walk in her dreams in order to uncover a hidden truth: a gift no one knew Greeta possessed. A gift that could make the world a better place.

"She meant how you can turn into a dragon," the Southlander said. "That's the gift."

"Maybe," Frayka said. "Maybe not." She turned to stab another vegetable out of the stew and then gestured with her dagger at Greeta. "Carry on."

Greeta hesitated, not sure she should tell them how she easily learned how to enter the Dreamtime and walk in it, meeting ghosts of her mother's past who offered their help and briefly meeting the mother she'd longed for but never known. Deciding to leave that fact out, Greeta told the truth, "One morning I woke up and the shaman was gone."

"Gone?" Erik said, suspicion in his voice.

Greeta nodded. "I looked for her everywhere but I couldn't find any trace of her. I found a village of Shining Star people, but instead of helping me, they captured me."

Several of the men nodded knowingly. One of them said, "I told you Vinelanders are demons." He shuddered. "So dangerous."

Greeta paused, astonished that Northlanders, the tallest and strongest people she'd ever seen, could be so frightened of people who were smaller and weaker.

Then again, when she and her family had first arrived on the shores of the Great Turtle Lands, Uncle Killing Crow had been lying in wait, ready to butcher them all.

The man who had spoken gestured toward Greeta. "Continue with your story."

"Those people sent me to a place. I'd never seen anything like it before." Greeta hesitated, wondering again how much to tell them.

But that's where it happened. That's where I turned into a dragon. Northlanders know about dragons, and they say they know about shapeshifters, too. What if they can help me figure out how to control changing between mortal and dragon?

Greeta closed her eyes, remembering what it looked like. "They took me to a settlement with cows grazing in a field. Most people lived in simple homes by a sheer stone cliff. But the cliff had been carved into a mansion full of rooms and hall-ways."

When the men whispered, Greeta open-ed her eyes, startled by their dark tones.

"Was there a man in charge?" Erik said, his voice even darker than those of the others.

"Yes. A Northlander. Like my family, he'd been living among Shining Star peo-ple for many years except not as one of them. He treated them like servants in-stead."

Erik's arms dropped to his side, and he clenched his fists unaware his strength made them crumble. "Did he have dra-gons? Or the eggs of dragons?"

Stunned, Greeta found herself speech-less. When she regained her wits, she said, "Yes! He kept a dragon imprisoned along with many eggs."

"Finehurst!" Erik hissed, clenching his fists so hard that they broke apart and fell to the ground.

CHAPTER 19

Greeta stared at Erik. "How do you know of Finehurst?"

Frayka said, "Who's Finehurst? You never said anything about another Northlander living in the Land of Vines!" When she turned to stab the stew again, one of the men passed down the bowl full of stew they'd first offered to her.

"A scoundrel!" the Southlander said.

"A traitor!" the man sitting on the other side of Frayka said.

"He's a berserk man," Erik said. "Finehurst knows right from wrong and doesn't care. All he cares about is himself." The color of his fiery eyes subdued to a cool blue. "Northlander Girl, you do not understand how lucky you are to still live."

Greeta's thoughts spun like a ship in a storm. "How do you know Finehurst?"

One of the men snorted, and small bits of gravel flew out of his nose. "He's the one who betrayed us! He's the reason we're here."

"He came as a servant to soldiers obeying a man who invaded our lands," Erik said. "All of us banded together. We planned to infiltrate the invader's camp where we could learn about the leader."

"We met in secret at my home," the Southlander said. "Finehurst was nothing but a servant, scuttling about. He overheard us and pretended to be one of us."

"But he was the infiltrator," another man said. "He infiltrated us before we could infiltrate them."

"I had a tapestry in my home," the Southlander continued. "Passed down from generation to generation. It told the story of my family and our history. But the tapestry makers must have embedded magic in it. Magic that stayed dormant until I invited a shapeshifter into my home so she could heal after being injured by a dragon while protecting me and my family."

"A shapeshifter?" Frayka sat up taller, paying close attention. She pointed at Greeta. "Like her?"

Greeta searched her memory. *Why does this sound familiar?*

"He used it against us," Erik said. "He must have found a local sorcerer or alchemist who told him how to harness the magic hidden inside, because the thing jumped off the wall. It wrapped around all of us, squeezing the life out of us."

"Thank the gods my family escaped," the Southlander said. "But he left us to rot outside my home."

"And that's when the Great Awakening came," another man said. "Finehurst brought us here with him. He used the tapestry to make us into what we are today. He tried controlling us, but it's the one thing that wouldn't work. So he bound us to this place with the condition that only the living could set us free. You're the first living people to find us." The man turned with hope toward Erik. "Doesn't that make us free to leave, Erik?"

"That it does," Erik said, somber and still. "Those gossiping trees finally did something useful."

Greeta gazed at the dozens of men before her, all dead and seemingly trapped in these strange forms. Their lives stolen from them. She remembered how Erik had just described Finehurst.

A berserk man. All he cares about is himself.

She remembered how Finehurst had held her in his arms and kissed her. How he'd talked about taking Greeta as his wife and taking her to their future marriage bed.

Greeta remembered her initial attracttion to Finehurst and how she thought he might be her only chance at love. That disturbing thought made her knees buckle, and Erik reached out to steady her before she could fall.

"He hurt you, too," Erik said, standing so close she could feel the warmth from his eyes.

Not wanting to reveal her past weakness, Greeta changed the course of conversation. "What is the Great Awakening?"

This time, Frayka answered. "Something that balanced countries that had gone out of balance. Too many bad men forced their beliefs on the Northlands,

Midlands, and Southlands. They killed people and controlled the lands. So the gods did what they had to do." She paused. "They killed everyone in those lands so those who escaped could start anew. Our people waged battle to keep the invaders from destroying the rest of the world. The gods used the forces of the sea, wind, and earth to cleanse the lands."

Greeta felt sickened and enlightened at the same time. "My mother. She stayed behind when my family sailed across the sea. The gods must have killed my mother just because she was in their path."

Papa claims he spoke to a god. That must have been before the Great Awakening happened. Did he know my mother would die if she stayed behind? Did Papa let it happen?

Then Greeta remembered why the tapestry seemed so familiar. "I've seen it," she said. "Finehurst had a tapestry hanging inside his mansion."

Erik spoke with a hush in his voice. "That tapestry is still full of magic."

Greeta remembered how she'd discovered a dragon and a cache of eggs trapped in Finehurst's complex. "Enough magic to control dragons?"

"Yes," the Southerner said. "And anyone with the power to control dragons can destroy what's left of the world."

CHAPTER 20

"I have to go back to the Great Turtle Lands," Greeta said, feeling panicked. "I have to find Finehurst. I have to stop him."

"Fine," Frayka said. "I will face the sorcerer alone."

Greeta pushed her panic away so she could think clearly. She remembered her decision to help Frayka. She'd made that decision after carefully considering how it could impact the next seven generations. Panicking would solve nothing. It made more sense to stick to her plan to stay by Frayka's side. But first she had to convince Frayka. "Maybe I should wait until after we find the sorcerer."

"No need," Frayka said. She made a shooing motion. "Go back home."

Greeta looked at Erik and his men. "They talk of strange magic, something far more powerful than an ordinary sorcerer. What if the sorcerer is Finehurst? What if he left the Great Turtle Lands after I discovered his secret stash of dragon eggs and has returned to the Land of Ice?"

The men made of rock and wood and moss gathered around the women, frenzied and speaking at once of the possibility of Finehurst's presence in the Land of Ice.

Erik stood next to Greeta. "You said you were imprisoned by Finehurst. How did you free yourself from him?"

Greeta met his gaze. "I turned into a dragon."

Erik cocked his head so far to one side that it threatened to fall off his shoulders. Another man caught Erik's head before it tumbled to the ground and pushed it back in place. "And you don't know how?"

"He made me angry," Greeta said.

"But you've been angry since and kept your mortal form." Frayka crossed her arms, boredom in her voice.

Erik pointed at Greeta. "She'll go nowhere until we learn the truth."

"I'm happy to tell you anything you want," Greeta said.

Erik gave her a steady gaze. "Tell us when you last saw him. And more about how you got away."

"He acted like he could control me," Greeta said. "When I was in mortal form and then again when I was a dragon. He had me tied up, but I wrenched myself free. I didn't realize it, but some friends had followed my tracks and were lying in wait for a chance to help me." Greeta smiled wistfully, torn between the sadness of having learned Wapiti didn't love her and the joy of discovering that three of his brothers had come searching for her. "I freed myself, and my friends helped me escape. We hid when Finehurst and his men came looking for us."

Although it had happened mere weeks ago, Greeta struggled to remember how it felt to be a dragon. How her mortal feelings had faded and she'd become more of a primal thing. "When I was a dragon, I wanted to destroy Finehurst. I went back to his mansion, but he and his people had vanished. I became mortal again, but I don't know how or why."

"When he left," the Southlander said, "did he take the tapestry with him?"

Greeta strained to recall what she saw when she'd lumbered through Finehurst's mansion in her dragon body. "I don't know. I can't remember."

Erik turned toward the Southlander. "You think the tapestry might have something to do with her turning into a dragon?"

"Could be," the Southlander said. "I've seen pictures of dragons on the tapestry along with mortals. Could even be some dragon magic embedded in the cloth."

Erik gestured toward Greeta. "You saw the tapestry and turned into a dragon."

"Not right away." Greeta shrugged. "A few days later, I think."

"You went back to the place where you saw the tapestry," Erik continued. "Let's say Finehurst took it with him. What if its presence turned you into a dragon and its absence turned you back into a mortal?"

Greeta considered it as a possibility but didn't feel convinced. "What if Finehurst came back to the Land of ice with his tapestry?"

"We don't know it's the tapestry that turned you into a dragon," Frayka protested. "And besides, we've had problems with ice dragons for much longer than a few weeks. How do you explain that?"

"*Ice* dragons?" Erik said.

The strange men nudged each other and spoke in whispers.

"What if Finehurst is in league with the sorcerer?" Greeta said. "Or what if Finehurst was once here, conjured up the ice dragons as guardians to make sure no one came near his palace, and now he's returned?"

"Palace," one of the men whispered.

"The ice castle," Frayka said to clarify. "That's where I'm going to find the sorcerer that has been plaguing my people and make him stop."

"And what if the sorcerer is Finehurst?" Greeta said. "I have to stay with you in case it's him."

Erik gestured to his companions. "And we would be most happy to accompany and help you."

The men pressed forward, talking excitedly.

Frayka cast a suspicious glance at

them. "What's in it for you?"

When Erik smiled, Greeta noticed he had black jagged shards of rock instead of teeth, making him look like a dangerous animal.

"If you're hunting Finehurst down," Erik said, "then you probably want to kill him. After all he's done to us, we'd be happy to help."

Greeta wondered if allowing Erik and his men to join them would change their journey in a good or bad way. The women barely knew these strange creatures. How could anyone predict what living men could do, much less dead ones? They might be dangerous.

Greeta turned toward Frayka and whispered. "I'm not so sure this is a good idea."

Frayka kept her voice low. "Think of all we've been through so far. How close we've already come to death." Frayka shrugged. "I say we let the dead men come with us. Safety in numbers."

"But the gossiping trees spread the word to them that we were coming," Greeta whispered. "And have you forgotten so quickly that they were planning to have us for dinner?"

176

Frayka laughed. "You may be a North-lander by blood, but you don't know how to be one. The key to survival is to shift with the wind and take whatever allies you can get." She cleared her throat. "And you forget that I'm the one with the portents. I'm the one supposed to make this journey. I've simply allowed you along for the ride." Turning toward Erik and his men, Frayka said, "We'd be happy to have you come with us."

Greeta struggled to smile, determined not to let the strange men see her fear of them. She reminded herself that Finehurst was a man far more dangerous who posed some kind of threat to her people. If she could find and stop him here in the Land of Ice, perhaps she could keep that threat from happening.

In addition to her resolve to help Frayka for the sake of the seven generations, she saw another way to protect the Shining Star nation. By traveling with Erik and his men, Greeta would have the opportunity to learn more about Finehurst and maybe even how he could be defeated.

She might even be able to learn more about dragons.

Erik's smile broadened. "We will be most happy to accompany you fine Northlander ladies to the ice castle."

Despite all the silent arguments she'd used to convince herself this was a good idea, Greeta noticed the gnawing feeling of dread that sank its teeth into her heart.

CHAPTER 21

Greeta found traveling with a pack of dead men to be very peculiar. Leading the way with Frayka, Greeta couldn't help but glance behind, curious to see how their companions would keep up.

In the confines of the towering black formations, shadows disguised the men and they seemed more like living mortals. But in the harsh light of the sun, they blended in with the landscape more easily. Each man had taken the shape of a mortal, but in the sunlight he looked more like a moving column of bits of rock and wood and plant, all seemingly held together by the invisible thread of his ghostly spirit.

After leaving the towering black formations, they crossed a field that stretched north for days, its long blades of grass rippling like a bright green sea in the wind. Far to the west, the land stood barren, comprised of nothing more than black rocks. Far to the east, they sometimes caught glimpses of the sea. Up ahead, a few dozen wild sheep scattered across the green field, their bleating breaking the silence.

Erik agreed to walk several paces in front of the women in order to detect hidden fissures. Every so often he'd sink knee deep into one, gesturing for the others to halt until he wrangled himself out of it and found solid ground. One time he stepped into a crevice so large that he sank into the grass, which appeared to swallow him.

Greeta and Frayka kept still.

Minutes later, Erik threw chunks of himself out of the crevice. Finally, Erik's rocky hands emerged above the waving grass. He hauled his head and upper torso out of the crevice with his arms and collapsed onto the ground.

"Erik," Frayka called to him. "Are you all there?"

"I'm fine," Erik said. His disembodied hands crawled and gathered up other pieces of himself. The hands dragged those pieces back to his intact head and torso to reattach them. A few times he hesitated, not seeming sure to which part of his body each piece previously belonged. "Give me a moment and I'll be good as new."

Greeta couldn't help but stare. Like the ice dragons, there seemed to be nothing holding Erik's body together. Even though he would jam a body part in place (although not necessarily the place it had previously been), that part didn't so much attach as float in place like seaweed on the ocean's surface.

After reassembling himself, Erik stood but looked different. His height had shortened and his torso had gained breadth. But he didn't seem to mind or even notice. Avoiding the crevice into which he had fallen, Erik made his way around it and created a new path for everyone to follow.

Greeta lagged behind, catching Frayka's attention. Frayka stopped and waited for her to catch up while the dead men forged ahead. "Are you hurt?" Frayka said.

Keeping her voice low, Greeta said, "No. They make me nervous."

"Well," Frayka said. "They *are* dead, and yet they're moving and talking. That should make anyone nervous."

"Do they make you nervous, too?"

"Let's not forget they were going to eat us. But if we hadn't agreed to let them come with us, I'm not convinced they would have let us go."

Frayka's words both reassured and chilled Greeta to the bone. Greeta whispered, "They remind me of the ice dragons."

Frayka nodded. "I noticed that as well. The difference is that they're made of earthly things instead of frozen water. And there's too many of them for us to fight." She readjusted the dagger lying in wait under her belt. "They said they want to find Finehurst, but those horrible gossiping trees probably told them where we're going. Or they guessed it."

Greeta swallowed hard. Frayka seemed to be on the verge of confirming Greeta's worst fear.

Frayka glanced at her. "If they're like the ice dragons, that means they might be servants of the same sorcerer. They know we're searching for that sorcerer. And now they'll make sure we find him."

Greeta wished she could turn into a dragon this moment. If she could take her dragon form, Greeta could thrash her tail at the dead men and dismantle them if they decided to try to make the women their dinner or come up with some other mischief. They'd stand no chance against her.

Maybe it's a matter of will. Maybe all I have to do is wish myself into a dragon.

Focusing with all her might, Greeta remembered how it felt to be a dragon. How it felt to be wild and primal.

A piercing bleat interrupted her concentration. Up ahead, a few sheep stood in their path.

Startled, Greeta realized the dead men had disappeared. "Where did they go?"

Frayka came to a halt. "They're still here. You didn't notice what they did."

Greeta stopped by Frayka's side, turning to look in every direction and seeing nothing but the rocky field to the west, a glimpse of the sea to the east, and the field behind and before them. "I don't see them anywhere."

"I think," Frayka said softly, "this is how they hunt." She nodded toward the sheep.

Baffled, Greeta took another look at the sheep, scattered across the field and grazing on the long blades of grass, ripping them, chewing them. Stepping over the low piles of rocks stretched all around them.

Rocks.

One sheep looked up when a pile of rocks behind several other sheep shifted.

The other sheep continued grazing, oblivious to the world around them.

When the pile of rocks crept forward, the one sheep took skittish steps backward. Alarmed, it looked all around, startled to discover another pile of rocks within inches of its feet. With a loud and distressed bleat, the single sheep leapt away just as those rocks reached for it. Finding itself free, the lone sheep raced toward the distant sea.

The other sheep looked up at the sound of the distressed bleat and began to scatter.

Greeta thought she felt a slight tremor beneath her feet.

And then everything happened so quickly that she thought the tremor must have been something caused by the dead men as a signal to each other.

The dead men raised themselves to full height in an instant, surrounding a few sheep and hurling themselves upon the animals. The attacked sheep screamed, gashed and torn apart by the sharp edges of the rocks.

The remaining sheep scrambled into a pack and ran away, keeping wide of the killing rocks, screaming sheep, and sprays of blood.

Greeta looked away. Back home, she was used to eating mostly nuts, berries, and vegetables from the fields that Papa planted and tended. Sometimes men from her village would bring back a deer or other animal from their hunt, but Greeta had never seen an animal killed before. The Shining Star people had taught her to respect animals and understand them to be brothers and sisters. And to thank every hunted animal for giving up its life in order to sustain the lives of the mortals who killed it.

Frayka nudged her. "What's wrong?"

Greeta felt light-headed. "The way they're killing. They're dead. I don't see how it's possible for them to eat."

"Maybe they can't. Maybe they're doing it out of habit. Or for sport." Frayka tilted her head, watching the slaughter. "Or maybe they like adding more bits to themselves."

"I've never seen anything like it."

"Me either," Frayka said, still facing the violent scene. "It's fascinating."

Looking at Frayka in horror, Greeta said, "It's disturbing!"

Frayka returned her look, although Frayka's face slackened with pity. "What did those Vinelanders do to you?"

"They taught me how to respect all living creatures." Speaking her truth made Greeta feel stronger and defiant.

"They squashed the Northlander right out of you." Frayka sighed, returning her gaze toward the bloody field. "But maybe I can help you figure out who you really are."

Greeta turned her back and walked away until the troubling sounds of ripping flesh were easy to ignore. She focused on the clarity of the sky above, the fresh wind in her face, and the way the grass swirled around her legs.

After awhile, she heard Erik call her name. She glanced back to see the dead men had reassembled themselves.

Walking back toward them, Greeta saw the remainder of the killing scene. Blood darkened a wide swath of the grassy field, and all that remained of the sheep were bits of wool and piles of bones.

But Greeta also noticed that some of the dead men had incorporated some of the bones among the rocks that formed their bodies. One man now wore a patch of bloodied wool on top of his head as if it were hair.

Approaching Erik, Greeta saw that he now wore what seemed to be the shoulder blades of the sheep like armor on his own shoulders. The pale bones still glistened with blood. When Erik grinned, she saw a tuft of wool stuck in his rocky teeth.

"Now that we're refreshed," Erik said, "we should move on."

Stifling her fear and disgust, Greeta said, "Lead on."

Once again, she lagged behind with Frayka. Whispering, Greeta said, "What I don't understand is what happened to the rest of the sheep."

"They ran away."

"No. The ones they attacked."

"They ate them."

Baffled, Greeta said, "How? These men don't have real bodies. Where did the parts they ate go?"

"You'd know that already if you'd had the courage to watch." Frayka smiled and then seemed to take pity once again. "I don't know exactly what happened, but they absorbed the sheep. I found it peculiar. And utterly fascinating."

Greeta shuddered. "Poor sheep."

Frayka laughed. "Better the sheep than us."

Greeta shuddered again, wondering how long it would be before the dead men preferred mortal flesh and bone instead of sheep.

CHAPTER 22

Greeta and Frayka traveled with the dead men for days toward the distant ice castle. Days became weeks, and weeks turned into months.

With every month that passed, the sun travelled lower in the sky, rising later and setting earlier. Dawn and twilight lingered until most of the day seemed dimly lit.

Wild sheep roamed in plentiful herds throughout the countryside. When the dead men killed the animals they often tossed a leg to the women. The farther they travelled north, the more the climate chilled, so the men saved sheep skins for the women to wear as cloaks. Erik and his companions would often reminisce about their mortal days.

"Mutton was fine," Erik said one evening while roasting sheep he'd given to the women for their supper. "But I miss potato stew with herbs and nuts."

"Potatoes?" a fellow dead Northlander said. "How can anyone miss potatoes of all things? They're bland and tasteless."

"Not the way my wife made them." Erik's voice became soft and wistful. "She kept a garden of every herb I'd ever carried home from other lands, not to mention herbs native to the Northlands. Every time she made her potato stew, she'd gather every herb growing in that garden and put it in the pot along with plenty of fresh milk and cream. They made the stew spicy and complex."

"Complex?" said the Northlander sitting next to him.

Erik spoke as if educating the uninformed. "There were layers to the flavors. First, there might be a spike of heat, not the kind where the food is warm from cooking but the kick from a strong pepper. Then there might be a sweetness or a savory taste. And that would go on and on after every bite."

"I miss our cooks," the Southlander said. "They made wonderful dishes with meats and vegetables. Not just mutton but beef and pork and chicken. Our vegetable gardens had all manner of greens and root vegetables. Even had rumbleberry bushes and sweet dove pip vines."

The dead man sitting next to Greeta whispered to her, "Had to be a rich bastard to afford all that, didn't he?"

By now Greeta had heard many of the dead men's stories. Everyone knew the Southlander had been wealthy, and some of the Northlanders resented him for that. She didn't care. Greeta's idea of wealth was having friends who proved their worth by helping her when she needed it and a loving family. As long as she had decent shelter to protect her from the elements and enough food to keep her sustained, she longed for little else. Although she still gave thought to someday finding a man she could love. A man who could give her children.

Months ago, she'd been able to think of little else. These days, it had become something she rarely had time to consider because more important things were at stake. For now, she agreed with Frayka that finding the sorcerer and confronting him was the most immediate way to keep their families safe from further attack.

That had to come first.

"I don't miss no potatoes none," another Northlander said. "But I do miss beef. Why ain't they got no cattle in this Land of Ice?"

"Too cold," the Southlander said.

"Can't grow the right kind of feed," another dead man said.

"Too skittish to be brought over on ships," Erik said, ending the argument.

Within days they reached a glacier where the ground became a blend of ice and gravel. Hills of ice surrounded them, reminding Greeta of the enormous chunks of ice that the sea sometimes deposited on the beach in the Great Turtle Lands after a harsh winter.

"Look," Erik said to Greeta and Frayka. He pointed between two hills of ice. "That's our way to the castle." Although it stood high enough on a hill to be seen from a distance, the only path required them to climb other hills above it.

Until now, the castle had looked like little more than a tall slab of ice, gleaming in the sunlight. Now they were close enough to get a better look, and Greeta marveled at its detail. Carved from ice, it stood several stories high, turrets anchoring each corner. Pale yellow light illuminated its many windows, some tall and narrow, others small and shaped like flowers. A thin moat of bubbling molten fire surrounded the castle. Steam and black smoke curled up from the bright orange lava.

Greeta shivered with fear and apprehension, noticing no movement, no sound near the castle. Except for the light glowing from within its walls, she would have thought it deserted.

"Careful," Erik announced to them all. "After climbing uphill all day we're now heading down. Should you lose your footing, there's no telling what lies ahead."

The dead men dug their rocky feet into the ice to get traction while Greeta and Frayka followed the patches of gravel that flanked their path. Greeta still carried the unfinished sword that she had been watching Papa forge when the ice dragons attached the Northlander settlement. But Erik had insisted she needed to take better care of it. Removing part of his knee, he'd used it to grind away some rust that had accumulated. He then made a simple sheath out of sheepskin with the wool on the inside where the sword could nestle against it. He explained the natural oil in the wool would protect the metal.

Just like the grassy land, deep crevices spread across the glacier like scratches made by the claws of gods. But without grass to hide them, these crevices were obvious and easy to avoid.

Now that the ice castle seemed within easy reach, Greeta wondered what Frayka had in mind. Walking next to her, Greeta said, "What's your plan to get into the castle? What if it doesn't belong to the sorcerer? What if it belongs to someone else? Or no one?"

"There's one way to find out." Frayka kept her eyes on the ground, mindful of every step. "Knock on the front door."

Stunned by the answer, Greeta said, "That's your plan?"

"Sure," Frayka said. "Why not?"

"Why not?" Even more astonished, Greeta struggled to understand Frayka's thinking. "If this sorcerer can create ice dragons to attack your people and a water witch that tried to kill us, don't you think knocking on his door might be dangerous?"

"We're not meek and mild girls from the Southlands. We're Northlanders. I have a knife and you have a sword." Frayka grinned, pulling her sheepskin tight around her shoulders. "And we have a lot of friends."

"Friends?" Greeta said in a harsh whisper. "These creatures might have been Northlander men once, but they're not who they used to be. They're dangerous!"

Frayka turned to face her with a raised eyebrow. "You think they weren't just as dangerous when they were mortal?" Shaking her head, she said, "Those Vinelanders made you forget what being a Northlander means."

Before Greeta could respond she felt the gravel shift and roll under her feet. She struggled to keep her balance.

Frayka cried out, losing her same battle with balance, and fell.

The glacier trembled, scattering the gravel to reveal a solid sheet of ice beneath it.

Another tremor made Greeta fall, and

sent both women sliding down the slope of the glacier.

Greeta cried out in surprise, twisting and reaching her hands out in hope of grasping anything that could stop her from sliding, but only emptiness surrounded her.

Looking back, she saw the sword and its sheath resting on the gravel behind and realized her fall had knocked them loose.

She heard Frayka call out for Erik.

Wincing at the bumpy glacial surface that dug into her body as she tumbled down its long slope, Greeta turned her head, looking for Frayka. Spotting her sliding slightly behind and to one side, Greeta reached out and called, "Take my hand!"

"Too far away!" Frayka shook her head and pointed at Greeta. "Keep your feet up!"

Greeta took quick note of the way Frayka slid on her side with her knees bent and feet lifted. Copying her, Greeta shifted from lying on her back to her side, facing Frayka while the world sped by them. She noticed Frayka looking forward and followed her gaze.

While Greeta's path stood open and clear, Frayka's downward slide was blocked by a boulder.

"Frayka!" Greeta cried out.

"Quiet!" Keeping her eye on the boulder, Frayka kept her knees bent and let her feet skim across the boulder when she met it. Seeming to dance along the boulder's surface, Frayka pushed against it and propelled herself across the ice toward Greeta.

Nearly colliding, Greeta managed to catch Frayka's hand while they sped down the glacier. Their momentum took them up onto a curving embankment that changed their path and sent them hurtling toward an open crevice.

"Hold on!" Frayka shouted. "Don't let go, no matter what!"

Greeta felt Frayka inch her grip upwards until she wrapped her fingers around Greeta's wrist. Following Frayka's lead, Greeta held on tight to her companion's wrist.

Frayka used her free hand to pull her dagger out from beneath the belt keeping it in place. With a white-knuckle grip, she stabbed at the ice repeatedly. While it slowed their momentum slightly, Frayka's stabs also helped control the direction and sent them toward solid ice at one end of the crevice.

Safety.

But as they rapidly approached, Frayka stabbed again at the ice and sent herself over the edge of the crevice, while Greeta slid past on solid ice, both women digging their fingers into each other's wrists.

Greeta's momentum took her over the edge of the glacier that she hadn't realized was there. Feeling the bone of her upper arm pop out of the shoulder socket, Greeta cried out in pain but still held onto Frayka.

Waves of pain threatened to make Greeta black out, but she focused on Frayka's voice, realizing her fall into the end of the crevice must have been calculated. Frayka must have recognized the edge beyond the crevice as a drop.

Looking down, Greeta saw that she hung over the edge of an ice cliff. The ground stood perilously far below, dotted with jagged rocks.

No one could survive such a fall.

When Greeta tried to tighten her grip on Frayka's wrist, her fingers didn't respond. She couldn't feel them.

The narrow stretch of solid ice between the crevice and the edge of the cliff shuddered with a loud crack.

It's going to break open. And when it does, we'll both fall.

As if reading her mind, Frayka shouted, "Don't give up!"

The crevice groaned and trembled.

Rocks hurtled past Greeta, and she ducked her head against the side of the cliff to protect it. She fought back tears, wishing she could have seen Papa and Auntie Peppa again, worried that they'd never know what had become of her. Wishing she could have gone back to the Great Turtle Lands. Back to Red Feather.

"Climb!" Erik's voice growled by her feet.

Startled, Greeta looked down to see several rocks that had pierced the side of the cliff like steps. On the largest she recognized Erik's glowing eyes.

"Any time today would be fine," Erik said, "but before it's too late would be a good idea."

Quick to take his advice, Greeta scrambled up the rocks jutting from the cliff side. Hurling herself over the edge and still clinging to Frayka, she discovered the dead men had caught up with them, disassembled themselves, and formed a rock path leading to the other side of the slope, covered in gravel. One had joined Frayka inside the crevice and created similar steps for her to climb.

Together, the women stepped onto the rock path and ran toward the gravel patch. The pieces of the dead men followed. They reached safety just as the crevice broke open and the cliff side fell apart, reshaping that part of the glacier. Still grasping Frayka's wrist, Greeta dropped to the gravel.

"Lie down," Frayka said, standing above her. Dagger still in hand, she placed it back under her belt.

Greeta wrinkled her face in confusion.

"Your shoulder popped out of place. I'll put it back where it belongs."

Still light-headed from the pain, Greeta followed Frayka's direction. Moments later, she cried out at the pain when Frayka made good on her word.

"It hurts now," Frayka said. "But you'll

feel better soon."

"You forgot something," the Southlander said, joining them. Kneeling next to Greeta, he smiled and placed the unfinished sword in its sheath by her side.

Greeta wrapped her hand around the sheathed sword, but the overwhelming pain in her shoulder made the world go black, and she lost consciousness.

CHAPTER 23

Greeta woke up to find herself standing alone on the glacier, still gripping her unfinished sword in its sheath. Taking a deep breath to keep her panic in check, Greeta called out, her breath fogging in the cold air. "Frayka! Erik!"

But her voice rang hollow between the hilly mounds of the glacier. When it faded, Greeta heard a tapping sound. She stayed in one place and turned slowly, searching for the source. She saw nothing but ice and gravel and gray sky above.

The tapping continued until Greeta felt it rise up into her body. Looking down, she realized the ice on which she stood had become thin as a leaf and transparent.

Someone stood on the other side of the ice beneath Greeta's feet, tapping against it.

Fear gripped Greeta's heart for a moment, making her want to run. She felt abandoned and threatened. If danger now threatened her, she had nothing but a rough and dull-edged sword for protection.

But then she noticed that the person beneath the thin sheet of ice on which she stood had long dark hair and the slight build of a woman.

"Frayka!" Greeta cried. No longer feeling any pain, Greeta took her sword out of its sheath and slammed its tip against the ice. Although thin and brittle-looking, the ice stood strong. Gripping her sword with both hands and holding it vertically and point-down in front of her, Greeta stabbed the ice repeatedly with the full force of her body behind each blow.

Cracks appeared, looking like a spider web as they spread around Greeta's feet. Encouraged, Greeta continued, drawing upon every ounce of her will to be strong and consistent.

Without warning, the ice broke apart and Greeta fell through it, still clutching her sword.

She landed, sprawled across soft grass.

Taking in her surroundings, Greeta realized she hadn't been abandoned by Frayka and the dead men because she wasn't in their world at the moment.

Instead, Greeta realized she now walked in the Dreamtime.

The woman who had appeared beneath the ice now smiled at Greeta. She looked nothing like Frayka but Greeta recognized her nonetheless.

"Your friend isn't here," said Greeta's mother, Astrid. Like Frayka, her hair was dark and long, her eyes just as dark. She offered a hand to help Greeta stand up.

Greeta accepted it, rising to her feet. "Frayka isn't my friend. She's just some-one I know."

Astrid laughed. "Once upon a time I felt that way about Margreet. And now she's my dearest friend."

Greeta took in her surroundings. She found herself in the center of a village's smithery on a warm summer day. A breeze brought the heat of the smithery fire against her skin. The Dreamtime had brought her to another country, another time, and another season.

When Astrid embraced her, Greeta noticed she smelled like smoke.

Letting go, Astrid took the sword out of Greeta's hands. "This looks like your father's work."

Defiance ran through Greeta's veins. Her father had always been there for her, raising her, protecting her, helping her. "Papa was teaching me how to make a sword."

"Something interrupted him. But you can finish it now."

"I'm not a blacksmith," Greeta protested, suddenly doubting herself. She knew so little that her inexperience would be obvious the moment she picked up a hammer. "I don't know how."

"You didn't know how to use a sword until Margreet taught you." Astrid walked into the heart of the smithery, surrounded by benches and tools.

She hurried to catch up to her mother's side. "Why have I entered the Dreamtime?"

"Elements surround us," Astrid said, ignoring Greeta's question. Holding up the sword, she continued. "The earth gives us the gift of iron. Air allows the fire to flame.

Fire heats the iron so we can forge it. And water quenches hot iron, giving it strength." She flipped the sword over and examined the other side of its blade. "Never forget how important these elements are to us. We can do nothing without them."

Crossing her arms, Greeta said, "Why can't anyone in the Dreamtime ever give me a straight answer? Why am I here? What's going on? You're my mother! You're the one who should help me the most."

Astrid met her gaze. "I don't know how to be a mother. I never knew you existed until it was too late."

"That's what I'm talking about!" Greeta said, jabbing an accusing finger at Astrid. "How can any woman not know she's giving birth?"

Astrid rested her hands on top of the anvil. "I entered a place that was something like your Dreamtime. I thought I was dreaming that I turned into a dragon and laid an egg that would later hatch under your father's care." Her eyes darkened. "When I left that place, I was mortal again. I never understood I had truly turned into a dragon. It never happened again."

Feeling light-headed, Greeta sank onto one of the benches. "That happened to me, but it happened in the mortal world, not the Dreamtime. I turned into a dragon. And I can't figure out how to do it again. Not when I want to. Not when I need to."

Astrid sat next to her on the bench. "Is that what you want? To be a dragon?"

Greeta remembered how her sense and sensibilities had changed when she'd been a dragon. How primal her thoughts had been. How she'd felt powerful and mighty. How she'd felt her humanity slipping away. "I don't know," she whispered.

"I wish I knew how to be a good mother to you," Astrid said, her voice soft and comforting. "I wish I could have been with you all this time."

Greeta's emotions rolled like ocean waves inside her. Relief to hear the words she'd always wanted to hear from the mother who had been absent throughout Greeta's life. Anger that she'd had to grow up without a mother. Fear of not having the immediate guidance she'd craved and that she didn't know how to be a woman as a consequence. Frustration of coming from a family torn apart, all because of the decisions her mother had made.

"But I can pick up where your father left off," Astrid said. "I can show you how to finish your sword. When you go back, you will have a perfectly sharp and polished sword, fit for a dragonslayer."

Astrid's offer wasn't enough to heal the pain of her absence from Greeta's life.

But maybe it could be a new beginning for the rest of Greeta's life.

"I'd like that," Greeta said. She knew her time in the Dreamtime would be un-predictable: it might feel like days or hours or even minutes. That unpredictable amount of time wouldn't make up for a lifetime bearing the absence of her mother.

But it would be a start.

Astrid faced Greeta, taking her hands in a tight grip. "Know this: whatever it is that binds you also has the power to set you free."

"I don't understand."

Astrid tightened her grip on Greeta's hands. "You will."

CHAPTER 24

When Greeta regained consciousness she found Frayka sitting next to her.

"She's awake!" Frayka called out. "Here," she said to Greeta, handing over her skin of water.

Greeta sat up and drank but winced in pain when she handed it back to Frayka. "My shoulder."

"I told you putting your arm back in place would hurt." Frayka took a sip of water and gazed back at the spot where they'd come close to a fatal fall. "But you're in one piece. We all are." Frayka's voice softened. "You're all right?"

Greeta considered the question. A life-time of longing for her mother had begun to ease. And although Frayka looked nothing like a typical Northlander, Greeta felt a comfort in feeling that perhaps she had found her own kind. "I'm all right," Greeta said.

She continued walking for another day with Frayka and the dead men across the glacier and up a gentle incline until they reached the ice castle, towering as high as a bird's flight. It stood like a fortress, defiant in the sunlight. Its walls glistened, reflecting sunbeams and casting prisms that appeared to dance across the glacial ground on which the castle stood. The many window panes were made of thin ice, distorting the yellowish light that came from within.

The group of travelers approached the moat of fire surrounding the castle. Molten and thick as stew, the fire bubbled noisily to the edges of the wide rocky trench that contained it. Greeta stared into its heart, bright yellow and orange. The fire reminded her of the colors that iron took when heated. Bits of thin black crust formed in patches and broke apart. The crust floated in the fire like bits of slag, the flakes of impurities hammered out of iron. Its acrid smell made Greeta's nose twitch.

Frayka balled her hands into fists and placed them on her hips. "Now what?"

"It's too wide to jump across," Greeta said. "But there has to be a way. Could we make a boat?" She looked hopefully at Erik.

He scoffed. "Out of us? We'd burn up and sink." He gestured at the barren landscape. "What would we use to build a boat? We got nothing but ice. Dirt. Gravel."

"What if we dumped all the ice and dirt and gravel we can find into the fire?" Greeta said. "Maybe it would fill up enough to make a path for us to walk across."

"The fire would spill out," Frayka said, shaking her head. "It would have nowhere else to go. And if the fire spills out, it melts the ground we're standing on."

"Worse than that," Erik said. He plucked a small stone from his neck and dropped it. The stone rolled down the incline, away from them. "We're on top of a rise. The fire spills out, it's going downhill in all directions. It'll run faster on ice that we can. No way to escape getting burned up alive by it." He paused when some of the dead men listening to him chuckled. Gesturing toward the women, Erik said, "For you, that is."

Greeta considered the moat that encircled the castle. "What if we walk around it?"

Frayka crossed her arms. "What will that get us?"

Pointing toward the left side of the castle, Greeta said, "The trench looks narrower over there. If we look for the narrowest spot, it might be easier to figure out a way to cross it."

Frayka nodded in agreement. "Then let's check all sides. I'll go the opposite way. We'll meet in back."

"Wait," Greeta said. "Why aren't there any guards? Why does it feel deserted?"

"There may be guards," Erik said, pointing toward the top of the castle enveloped by a thick haze. "They may be hiding up there. Or they might be spirit guards instead of living ones."

The dead men split up, half of their numbers joining each woman. Erik walked alongside Greeta as they followed the moat around the left side of the castle.

Since returning from her most recent

walk in the Dreamtime, Greeta had developed a habit of pulling her sword out of its sheath and checking it. In the Dreamtime, her mother Astrid had taught her how to finish the sword, and together they'd sharpened the edges and polished the blade until it shimmered, revealing a pattern running down its center that looked like dragon scales. They'd forged a crossbar, slid it over the tang, and then wrapped the tang in leather to create the sword's grip. Finally, they'd forged a pommel and welded it to the last bit of exposed tang, completing the weapon.

But that was in the Dreamtime.

Here in the real world, Greeta eased the sword slightly out of its sheath, and it still disappointed her. The blade looked dull and rough, and its tang stuck out like a naked thumb. No matter how many times she looked, it never changed.

Why should I believe the words of a mother who deserted me? How can I be so stupid to trust someone who I can meet only in my dreams?

"Something wrong with your sword?" Erik said, watching Greeta.

For a moment, she remembered what

Astrid had told her about the elements: the earth produces iron, the air helps fire come into existence, the fire heats the iron, and the water quenches it.

"No," Greeta said, letting the unfinished sword slide back in its sheath. "Nothing's wrong."

Looking over Greeta's head, Erik stared at the moat of fire. Shaking his head in disappointment, he said, "Even wider here."

Sidling up to Erik, another Northlander pointed at the moat and said, "Who could have created such a thing?"

Erik shook his head again, unable to answer.

Greeta motioned for them to follow her, and she circled the castle until she stood behind it. Pointing at the moat, she said, "Look. It's narrower here."

Frayka and the other dead men appeared from the opposite side and walked toward Greeta. "Not by much," Frayka said. "But better than anything we saw."

Greeta paced along the edge of the moat, grateful for the wave of heat arising from it. She considered all of their resources: ice, gravel, the sheepskin the dead men had given to each woman to use as a makeshift cloak. A dagger and an unfinished sword. If attacked they had little to protect themselves.

The sight of a rock soaring above her head startled Greeta. She watched its flight until it landed on the other side of the moat. Spinning around, she saw the Southlander pluck one hand off with the other and hurl it across the fire. His hand landed next to the first rock thrown, which Greeta now realized he had been using as a foot because one leg now ended in a stump.

"And that proves my point," the Southlander said, hopping in an attempt to keep his balance.

"What point?" Greeta said.

The Southlander beamed. "We'll throw ourselves over one chunk at a time. Reassemble on the other side. And do what we came here for."

"What about us?" Frayka said. "How are we supposed to get across?"

"No need," Erik said. "You stay here."

"No," Greeta said. "If some of you can hurl yourselves over, you can join forces to make a bridge on each side and then meet in the middle. Then we could walk across you."

Ignoring her, Erik called out to the dead men. "We cross here!"

"You can't all get across," Frayka argued. "Even if all you need is an arm to throw pieces of yourself, the arm can't throw itself. Someone has to stay behind."

Erik shrugged. "Or someone leaves his arm behind."

Frayka pulled her dagger from beneath her belt and waved it at Erik. "This is my portents! I'm the one to face the sorcerer! I'm the only one who can make things right! If you try it alone, you'll die."

The dead men paused and laughed.

Erik brushed away the threat of her dagger as if it were a butterfly. "You assume you're the only one with reason to be here." He gestured at the castle. "If it's Finehurst that be here, we got a score to settle with him."

"What if it's not Finehurst?" Greeta said, astonished. "What if it's a sorcerer?"

Ignoring her, Frayka became frantic. "Don't face the sorcerer without me! I have to be the one. It's in the portents!"

The Southlander scoffed. "We were supposed to have portents of living in a great hall in our mortal bodies. We were supposed to drink mead and laugh and sing until the day the world ended and the gods would join us." He gestured to his fellow dead men, composed of rock and wood and earth. "See what happened instead? We're here to make sure Finehurst gets what's coming to him."

"Enough," Erik said. "That's none of their business. Ours lies ahead of us." Pointing across the moat of molten fire, Erik shouted to his men, "Across!"

Frayka continued her protest while the dead men disassembled and threw themselves bit by bit across the moat.

Defeated, Greeta stepped back, mulling over what to do next.

Maybe the ice dragons meant to attack the dead men, not Frayka's settlement. Maybe her people were never in danger.

Erik has so many men, and no one can kill them because they're already dead. Whoever lives inside that castle stands no chance against them.

Despite Frayka's shouting, the dead men continued hurling pieces of themselves across the moat, helping each other gather up those pieces and put themselves back together on the other side. Eventually, only one Northlander remained, tossing the last bits of each man across before taking himself apart. After several throws, his legs supported part of a torso and one arm but no head. Gathered into a heap by his colleagues, he yelled, "Could you women throw the rest of me across?"

"Of course!" Frayka called out, still pacing next to him. Taking a calming breath, she tucked her dagger away. With great care she removed his entire arm and threw it into the fire.

"Hey!" the last Northlander cried. "That was uncalled for!"

Smiling in response, Frayka wrestled his torso into pieces and shoved them into the fire.

"Stop that!" the last Northlander said.

Before Frayka could touch them, his legs ran away, scuttling across the ice and circling back toward the front of the ice castle.

As if accepting a challenge, Frayka chased after them.

"Your friend," the last Northlander said to Greeta, "has some very serious problems in her head."

Taking offense, Greeta shouted back, "Maybe she doesn't like it when dead men lie to her." When no one responded, she watched each man pull a bit of himself free and donate it to the last Northlander until he had enough parts to compose himself.

Gazing up at the ice castle towering above them, the Southlander said, "Last time going through the front door did nothing but lead to disaster. How do we get in this time?"

"Last time?" Greeta called out. "Have you been here before?"

Erik pointed at the windows closest to the ground level. "The panes are thin. We can break them."

"But how?" the last Northlander to cross the moat said.

Erik grinned. "Use your head, man!"

Laughing, the dead men gathered by the windows. Each pulled his head from his shoulders and used it to bash against the thin ice forming windowpanes.

Cracking sounds filled the air, and the glacial ground shuddered beneath Greeta's feet.

More than ever, she wanted to go home. Not back to Blackstone but across the sea with Papa and Auntie Peppa. Back to the Great Turtle Lands. Back to the Shining Star people. Back to her beautiful, lovely beach made of soft, white sand, not the strange black sand that covered the shores of the Land of Ice. She wanted to be with the people who knew and cared about her, people who respected all life and lived in peace.

I can't do this anymore. I can't bear it. It's too much of a burden, and I don't have the strength to carry it anymore.

But if I don't see this through, terrible things could happen.

Something shifted inside Greeta. Her skin felt too tight to contain her body. Everything itched, but scratching brought no relief.

She flicked her tongue to taste the air. A peculiar tang in the air caught her attention.

Finehurst?

No one noticed Greeta.

The dead men crashed their heads against the windows made of ice.

Greeta sank to all fours and rested her

belly against the frigid ground. It seemed to relieve the itch. She closed her eyes and rocked her head from side to side. Her arms and legs felt heavy and thick. When she curled her hands, she felt her fingernails drag across the icy surface beneath her.

She remembered all the wild sheep they'd seen while walking through the Land of Ice. Greeta wondered what it would be like to hunt one.

This is what I've been waiting for! I'm about to turn into a dragon. This is how I felt before it happened.

And once I'm a dragon I can jump across the moat or maybe even walk through it.

The windowpanes made of ice shattered and fell away. Erik and his men climbed into the ice castle.

The sound startled Greeta. She felt the shift inside her reverse. Suddenly, the ground that had felt soothing moments ago now made her shiver. She stood and remembered how she thought she'd tasted Finehurst's scent in the air. The desire to find out whether or not Finehurst had taken refuge inside the castle overwhelmed Greeta.

Erik and his men know Finehurst.

What had they called him?

A scoundrel. A traitor. A berserk man.

Greeta remembered what Erik said.

Finehurst knows right from wrong and doesn't care. All he cares about is himself.

Erik had told Greeta she didn't know how lucky she was to still be alive after meeting Finehurst.

Erik's men claimed Finehurst betrayed them. The Southlander said Finehurst harnessed the magic in his family tapestry and used it to kill them. The dead men also blamed Finehurst for bringing them to the Land of Ice.

Greeta steeled herself.

I can help the Shining Star people and the Great Turtle Lands by learning as much as I can about Finehurst. We can better protect ourselves from him when we know more about him.

That matters far more than my longing for home.

From inside the castle came the muffled scream of a woman.

A woman! Has the sorcerer captured someone? Was that in Frayka's portents? Is that why confronting the sorcerer matter-

ed so much to her?

Anguished cries from the dead men echoed inside the castle for several minutes, and then the world fell silent.

CHAPTER 25

Fear crawled across Greeta's skin, anchoring her in place, unable to move. She wanted to call out, but every time she tried to shout, only a whisper came out of her mouth.

All of the windowpanes in the ice castle shattered at the same moment. Shards of thin broken ice that had formed those panes rained from the open windows.

The soft yellow light inside the castle escaped like the rays of the sun piercing through clouds. The light fell upon Greeta's face, warm and inviting.

But a loud booming sound from inside the castle extinguished the light.

Moments later, thick fog poured

through the castle, spilling onto the ground surrounding it.

Greeta found her voice. "Frayka!"

At the same time, Frayka rounded the curve of the moat on one side of the castle. She carried the escaped legs of the last Northlander, which struggled mightily in her arms. Within moments, she joined Greeta's side.

"Did you hear that woman scream?" Greeta said. "We have to get inside the castle to help her."

Frayka shifted her grip on the dead Northlander's legs, still squirming in her arms like a disgruntled toddler. "These might help. I just have to figure out how to use them."

A sense of dread overwhelmed Greeta. "This isn't right. None of this is right."

The fog spilled into the moat. When it touched the fire, the fog turned it to ice. Rolling slowly toward the women, they watched as each molten flame became solid.

Entranced by the sight, Frayka's grip relaxed. The legs wriggled free and ran away. This time, Frayka ignored them.

"It's coming toward us," Greeta whispered. "Should we get out of its path? Will it harm us?"

"Wait," Frayka said, staring at the oncoming fog. "This reminds me of a portents I had years ago. I never understood it. But now it's making sense."

Greeta backed away, but Frayka remained near the edge of the moat.

When the fog reached that edge and all of the molten fire had turned to ice, the fog dissipated. It turned to steam, rising from the ground and into the air where it formed a dark cloud.

Frayka smiled. "Problem solved." She stepped onto the frozen fire.

"Frayka, wait!" Greeta shouted, running toward her with an outstretched hand, ready to pull her back just in case something went wrong.

But Frayka had already taken several steps across the ice, its surface as uneven as boiling water. She held her arms out for balance and pushed one foot to glide on the other, skating around and through the unevenness.

Greeta followed Frayka onto the ice, hurrying to catch up.

Within minutes Frayka stepped out of

the moat and onto solid ground on the other side. She kicked some broken shards of windowpane out of her way.

"Wait!" Greeta called.

Frayka turned, looking surprised to see Greeta hadn't run away like the North-lander legs. "I'm not letting you hold me back. Waiting for you is costing me time. I told you I'm the one who has to face the sorcerer. It's in the portents."

"Fine," Greeta said. Her foot slipped out beneath her and she fell onto the icy fire. Climbing back on her feet, she said, "Do what you need to do. Talk to the sorcerer. I'll be here in case you need anything."

Heaving a heavy sigh, Frayka sounded as if she were burdened with a wayward child. But she stood by the edge of the moat and waited for Greeta. "Don't mess with my portents again."

Greeta took her time with each step, partly because she didn't want to fall again and partly because it gave her time to think. "I didn't mess up your portents."

"I should have been able to kill all the ice dragons myself. Instead, one got away and probably made it here to report to the sorcerer, who likely knows we're here.

That means I've lost the advantage of surprise."

Greeta slid another step. "We don't know the dragon made it here. We lost its tracks. It probably melted before it got here."

Frayka scoffed. "And then there's Erik and his merry band of the dead. If I'd killed all the dragons I would have taken the most direct route here, and I never would have met them. There's no telling how much damage they've caused inside."

"Or maybe they've made things easier for you. Maybe they've paved the way. Maybe you couldn't succeed without them."

"Nonsense." Frayka gave her hand to Greeta, helping her onto solid ground. "Watch for the broken ice."

The women picked their way through the shards of ice littering the ground and climbed through the same window that Erik and his men had used to enter the castle.

Once inside, the chill in the air hit Greeta like a slap.

Like the exterior, everything was made of ice: the floor, walls, ceiling, and furniture. The light coming from the outside gleamed off the icy surfaces, making the room bright. Greeta wondered what it must have been like before the warm light had been extinguished. Had it been blindingly bright?

A woman's moan echoed inside the castle.

"What if the sorcerer is holding a woman captive?" The sound made Greeta's stomach wrench, worried for the woman. "We have to help her."

Frayka nodded. "It's the surest way to find the sorcerer. If we set her free, he'll know. He'll come looking to find out what happened. I can ambush him."

"But we have to help her first."

Frayka gave Greeta a blank stare, seeming baffled. "Of course. That's obvious."

Not always certain of Frayka's intents, her words calmed Greeta, convincing her that despite Frayka's intense focus on her portents, she still kept important things in mind.

They explored the entire ground floor of the castle, finding no one. After climbing a winding staircase, they paused at the top of the next floor, finding themselves in a grand ballroom.

Tall windows lined the walls, making them and the floor and ceiling sparkle with light. Chairs made of ice stood in a single row against each wall. At the far end of the room, a small tapestry of an elegant woman hung on the wall.

Erik and his dead companions stood scattered across the ballroom floor, each looking as if he'd been caught in mid-step back toward the staircase. A thin layer of ice covered each man, keeping him in his place.

Frayka approached the nearest dead man, taking her dagger out from beneath her belt. Standing in front of him, she tapped the dagger blade lightly against his ice-covered nose. "I bet you wished you'd helped us now," she said, grinning.

Ignoring Frayka, Greeta took her unfinished sword from the sheath the dead men had made for her. She delivered a solid blow against his waist, knowing the sword couldn't harm him.

To her surprise, the sword bounced off as if the ice were made of steel.

Frayka sidled up to her and tapped the ice gently with the point of her dagger, careful not to damage her weapon. "Strong sorcery."

The moan filled the air once more.

Looking up, Greeta realized where the sound came from. Pointing across the room at the tapestry, she said, "I think that's her. I think she's trapped inside the tapestry."

"Or the sorcerer brought her to life inside it," Frayka said.

They crossed the room, weaving their way between the statue-like dead men. Squinting, Greeta struggled to understand what she saw on the wall. She then realized they hadn't been looking at a tapestry. They'd been looking at a real woman trapped inside the wall.

A woman stood inside a niche, separateed from the room by a wafer-thin sheet of transparent ice. Her long black hair flowed wild and free, billowing around her as if windblown. She blinked when she saw Greeta and Frayka. She strained to reach toward them, but her arms remained stretched out to either side because each hand had been bound and tied to a dagger impaled into the ice wall surrounding her.

Greeta withdrew her sword and struck a

blow against the thin sheet of ice in order to free the woman, but her weapon bounced off without causing so much as a crack. She stared at the sword, confused. "That should have broken the ice."

Frayka circled the niche, staring at the woman. "None of this was in the portents. It makes no sense."

Greeta thought back to every way Margreet had taught her to use this type of sword when they'd met in the Dreamtime. Sometimes Margreet had supplied gloves, which allowed Greeta to grip the blade itself, giving her not only more control but more options.

But that happened when I trained with an iron sword with sharp edges. This sword is unfinished! It can't hurt my hands if I grip it by the blade.

"Of course, I never saw the sorcerer's face in the portents," Frayka continued, lost in thought. "Only a dark figure. But this woman in the ice wasn't there."

Greeta placed one hand on the sword's tang and the other on its dull blade. Aiming its point at the sheet of ice standing between her and the captured woman, Greeta held the sword as high as her head and parallel to the ground. She jabbed the point at the ice.

The sword point pierced the ice but the sheet remained intact. Careful to avoid harming the captive woman on the other side, Greeta pushed the entire blade through the ice. Withdrawing it created a slim open space where it had punctured the ice. Encouraged, she continued, striking just below or above each previous puncture mark.

"It might be best to think about this first," Frayka said. "We don't know who this woman is. Or who put her there. Or why."

"What if it was you in her place?" Greeta said, continuing to puncture the sheet of ice, leaving an outline of marks like the seam line of thread a seamstress would leave in a dress. "What if you were the one who needed help?"

"What I'm saying is we don't know who or what she is. And I'm not entirely certain she's mortal."

"She looks mortal enough." Greeta continued, picking up speed and creating an outline in the shape of a door.

"So do you," Frayka said. "And yet you

claim you've taken the shape of a dragon."

Her words scared and enthralled Greeta at the same time. Greeta said, "Then maybe she's like me."

"By the gods," Frayka said. "Your hand. It's bleeding."

Greeta stopped, staring at her hands. Blood ran from the hand that gripped the blade, splattering onto the ice floor.

With a start, she realized the appearance of the sword had changed. The blade gleamed as if it had been polished. Its edges and point looked as if they'd been hammered to a fine sharpness. It seemed as if pushing the sword through the ice had sharpened and polished it, which made no sense. Unless the ice had been enchanted.

And the newly-sharp blade had cut the hand holding it.

Wincing from the pain she now felt in one hand, Greeta shifted both hands to grip the tang and delivered another blow against the ice.

This time, the door-like section that Greeta had outlined by piercing the ice broke apart, falling to reveal the woman trapped behind it.

"By the gods," Frayka said, dropping to her knees.

"Someone stuffed cloth in her mouth." Greeta stepped forward, taking hold of an edge of a narrow strip of cloth dangling over the woman's lower lip. She pulled with a gentle but steady force, hand over hand. The cloth seemed endless and piled up on the ice floor between Greeta and the captive woman. Finally, the last bit of cloth came free from the woman's mouth.

She coughed for a minute or so and struggled to catch her breath. Inhaling deeply, she stared at Greeta and hissed, "Scalding!"

CHAPTER 26

"By the gods," Frayka said with a trembling voice. "Leave her be!" She scrambled to her feet and wrapped a firm hand around Greeta's arm. "We have to get out of here!"

Greeta stared at the captive woman, baffled. "There is nothing scalding here. Nothing hot. Everything is cold."

"Scalding!" the woman hissed again, her eyes blazing with anger. "*You* are Scalding!"

"Actually," Greeta said, "I feel quite chilly at the moment."

"She means you're one of the Scaldings," Frayka said. Annoyed, she added, "Which you could have warned me about if you cared about anything other than your own safety."

Perplexed, Greeta said, "What are you talking about? What is a Scalding?"

"I know who you come from," the woman said. She sniffed the air and her manner softened for a moment. "You smell like her. Like past. Like pain. Like hope." She struggled but the cloth binding her wrists held tight. "Free me, Scalding! Or suffer consequences."

"There's no need to threaten anybody," Greeta said to the woman. She slid her sword back into the sheath at her side and then untied one of the cloth restraints. "The reason we came inside was to help you."

"No!" Frayka cried, lunging toward the restraint.

The cloth came undone with far more ease than Greeta would have imagined.

With one hand free, the woman tried to untie the other restraint but cried out in pain at the attempt. "Free me!" she commanded Greeta.

"Don't!" Frayka said, grabbing both of Greeta's hands, oblivious to the blood from where the sword's newly sharpened blade had cut Greeta's skin. "You don't know what she is."

"There's no need to be bossy," Greeta said to the woman. "I already told you we're here to help." She wrenched her hands out of Frayka's and untied the other cloth restraint.

Screeching, the woman pushed past them and onto the floor scattered with the bodies of Erik and his men frozen in place. Taking a deep breath, the woman exhaled toward them, her breath foggy in the cold. In an instant, the foggy breath formed a small cloud that rained a downpour, and the rain immediately formed a thin sheet of ice that pushed Greeta and Frayka into the niche where they had found the woman, now entrapping them in the same place.

Astonished, Greeta said, "Is that how you repay people who help you?"

The woman turned her back on them and ran out of the room, her feet skimming along the icy floor as if she were dancing across it.

"We're dead," Frayka said, her voice dull and without hope. "Now we're trapped and we're going to die here."

"No, we're not," Greeta said. Noticing the strips of the cloth on the floor that had bound the woman, she picked one up. It had more heft than most cloth and was covered with embroidery.

Like cloth cut from a tapestry.

Frayka banged her head against the ice sheet entrapping them. "None of this was in the portents. Everything went wrong. This wasn't supposed to happen. Why didn't you listen to me? I warned you!"

Greeta took one strip of tapestry and wrapped it around her bleeding hand, tucking the end to keep it in place.

"You do know what that was, don't you?" Frayka said, turning angrily toward Greeta. "That was a dragon god. They used to rule the Northlands." Frayka shouted, "Before they destroyed it!"

Greeta withdrew her sword from the sheath and examined it.

"She must be one of the water dragons." Frayka waved her hands all around. "That would explain all of this. Water. Ice. Rain. Fog. It's all having to do with water dragons."

Greeta took another strip of the tapestry and wrapped it around the tang of her sword to create a grip.

"It all makes sense now," Frayka said, drifting back to hopelessness. "We assumed a sorcerer made the ice dragons to drive us away, but there never was a sorcerer. It was a dragon goddess. She must have made those ice dragons to try to get our attention so someone would come and free her. She can probably make ice dragons with her mouth gagged and her hands tied."

Greeta wrapped both hands around the grip to test it. She moved her tapestry-wrapped hand around the blade, satisfied that the cloth protected her skin from its sharp edges.

"And the water witch!" Frayka said. "The dragon goddess probably conjured spirits in all the waterfalls. Maybe put them there as lookouts. That water witch wasn't trying to hurt us. She was hurrying us along! And I'll wager the spirits use those horrible gossiping skeleton trees to spread the news back to the dragon goddess."

Just as she had done from the other side, Greeta began piercing the thin sheet of ice entrapping them with her sword.

"Truly?" Frayka said, watching her. "You think that'll work again? You don't think the goddess included some enchantment in that ice that will keep us stuck here until we die?" Frayka heaved a cumbersome sigh. "Which will most likely be any minute now because we're going to run out of air."

Greeta withdrew her sword from the sheet of ice, happy to see the slim gaping hole it left behind. "We're not running out of air." Greeta repeated piercing the ice just as she had done before.

Ignoring her, Frayka leaned against the niche wall and slid down it until she sat on the ice floor. "I'll never have children. I'll never pass on my power of portents. How will my people survive?" She covered her face with her hands and wept. "It's your fault! You never should have come here! You should have left me alone with my portents. You've ruined everything!"

Greeta continued her task until she created a new outline of a door. Once again, she shifted both hands to the grip and struck a blow at the ice sheet.

But the barrier stood fast.

Wiping her tears away, Frayka's tone

became argumentative. "And your lies about who you are. How dare you keep such a critical secret from me?" Shaking her head in disgust, Frayka sang a children's rhyme:

Mind yourself
Mind your thoughts
Or Scaldings
Tie you into knots

They take you
Into their tower
Walk inside
Where dragons glower

Rip your head
Leave you for dead...

Greeta stared at Frayka. "I have no idea what you're talking about."

Frayka snorted. "As if you've never heard the story of the Scaldings."

Glancing at her, Greeta said, "I'm from the Great Turtle Lands." She paused, remembering the name that Northlanders used. "I'm from the Land of Vines. There's no story like that there." Taking another approach, Greeta slid the sword through one of the slits she'd made at the top of the outline. Placing both hands on the sword's grip, she wrenched it along the dotted outline she'd made to slice through it.

"*Everyone* knows about the Scaldings," Frayka said.

"Not the people of the Shining Star nation," Greeta said, eyeing the clean cut she had just made. Even though half of the outline was now a slim but gaping hole, the rest of the outline stood intact. Greeta tapped the point of her sword against the ice, testing its strength. It felt solid.

"But your family is from the Northlands, not the Land of Vines. They're Northlanders, not savages."

Ignoring the insult to the people she loved, Greeta placed her sword through the gap at the top of the outline. She wrenched the weapon in the opposite direction, cleaving the outline open to create a free-standing door. It trembled.

Greeta kicked the door, causing that part of the ice wall to fall forward. Now they had a way to escape. She stepped out of the niche where they'd found the woman and into the room dotted with frozen, dead Northlanders. "Let's go."

Startled at the realization that Greeta had freed them, Frayka said, "Go where?"

Greeta considered all they'd been through: being separated from the ones they loved when ice dragons created a chasm to erupt around Blackstone. Fighting ice dragons and escaping the witch when they crossed the waterfall. Walking through a shallow lake while trees gossiped on its shores, sending word to Erik and his dead friends. They'd helped a woman by setting her free even though Frayka protested that the woman was actually a dragon goddess.

Despite her longing to go back to the Great Turtle Lands, Greeta had made a commitment to stay in the Land of Ice until she, Papa, and Auntie Peppa had fulfilled their promise to help the Northlanders. After considering how her decisions might impact the next seven generations, Greeta had come to the conclusion that helping the Northlanders was the right thing to do and the best course of action.

But the ice dragons were gone and no longer posed a threat. The Northlanders had feared a sorcerer, but there was no sorcerer threatening them. Even if the woman they'd freed turned out to be a goddess, didn't the gods exist to protect mortals and the world in which they lived?

I kept my promise. I've done what I believe is right. It's over.

Overwhelmed by the events of the past few months, Greeta felt exhausted. She wanted to get her life back. She wanted to see her family. "We're going home."

Stepping outside the niche, Frayka hustled to keep up with Greeta. "Home? But what about my portents?"

"Do whatever you want," Greeta said, crossing the room. Glancing back, she saw Frayka pause next to Erik's frozen figure and remove the dagger from beneath her belt. With a sigh, Greeta pressed forward, weary of this strange Land of Ice and anxious to reunite with her father and auntie so they could return to the Great Turtle Lands.

CHAPTER 27

Winding her way through the ice castle, Greeta made her way outside to the moat of solidified fire, ready to walk across it and find her way back to the Northlander settlement.

Instead, she found the woman she had set free standing at the edge of the moat. The woman turned, pointing at Greeta and hissed at her again. "Scalding!"

Stepping up to face her, Greeta said, "I don't know why you keep saying that. My name is Greeta. And although I don't expect you to thank me for rescuing you, I would appreciate it if you'd stop saying that every time we meet." Greeta paused when the woman's face relaxed in surprise. "We haven't met properly. What is your name?"

"Norah." The woman scrunched up her nose as if disgusted by her decision to reveal her name. Turning her back on Greeta, Norah placed one foot on the moat. The area around her foot instantly turned back to flame. Screeching in pain, Norah turned back to Greeta and pointed at the flame. "Make it stop! I must cross!"

Astonished, Greeta knelt by the edge of the moat and watched the molten flame gradually turn back to solid form. "This didn't happen when we crossed it." Looking up at Norah, she said, "Some kind of fog rolled out of the castle. When the fog touched the fire, it turned flames to ice."

Norah stared at her for a long moment, her eyes squinting in puzzlement. Then she took a deep breath and exhaled. The same type of fog poured out of her mouth and spilled onto the ground and then onto the moat. Closing her mouth, Norah took a tentative step onto the icy moat.

But the moment her foot touched the ice, it turned back into flame. Norah cried out, pulling her foot back. "Trapped," she whispered. Turning to Greeta, Norah gestured to the ice castle. "Trapped!"

"I don't understand," Greeta said, puzzled. "We had no problem crossing the moat." Sitting down at the moat's edge, she placed a foot on its icy surface.

This time, no flames erupted. The moat's surface remained cold and hard.

Norah stared in wonder. Pointing at Greeta, she said, "Stand!"

Greeta placed her other foot in the moat and pushed off of the ground to stand.

Nothing changed. The moat remained icy beneath Greeta's feet.

"How?" Norah demanded.

Greeta shrugged. She sat on the edge, pulling her feet back before anything dangerous could happen.

The strip of cloth bound around Greeta's injured hand worked itself loose and crawled like a worm onto the moat's frozen surface.

"You might try using that," Erik shouted. "That's part of the tapestry Finehurst used against us."

Greeta turned to see Frayka walking toward them. She held Erik's head by his hair of vines and red berries. The rest of Erik's body was nowhere in sight.

"Evil!" Norah hissed, pointing at Erik's head. "Bad men!"

Rising to her feet and facing Frayka, Greeta said, "What have you done?"

Frayka lifted Erik's head up to eye level. "I see no reason to trust him after he ditched us on the other side of this moat. But he knows things. Getting here was difficult enough, and it might be just as difficult to get home. Why not let him help?"

"Liar!" Norah said, still pointing at Erik.

Frayka dropped to one knee, still holding Erik's head high. She spoke with reverence. "That may be, my goddess. But I made sure he has reason to tell the truth."

Norah stepped closer, glaring into Erik's fiery eyes. "What reason?"

"I left Erik's body behind. And all of his men. If he fails us in any way at any time, I promise to split his head apart and bury the pieces in different places throughout the Land of Ice." Frayka grinned. "He'd be trapped with no hope of being himself again."

"This isn't my fault," Erik said. "None of it."

Norah grabbed the cloth at the base of Frayka's throat and lifted Frayka to her feet. Still fixated on Erik's head, Norah said, "Tapestry is evil. Why should it help?"

"I believe Finehurst found an alchemist who told him how to harness the magic hidden inside the tapestry," Erik said. "Remember it's not us that brought the tapestry but Finehurst."

"Finehurst?" Greeta said. Looking from Erik's head to Norah, Greeta began piecing information together. "She knows Finehurst, too? That's why you and your men have been here before?"

Erik nodded and continued addressing Norah. "He released the magic inside the tapestry. Good and bad magic alike as far as I can tell. Remember that Finehurst used it against us, too."

"Evil man!" Norah said.

Even though Frayka insisted Norah was a dragon goddess, Greeta had seen no reason to believe it. For all she knew, that could be something Norah believed and had convinced others to believe it, too. Greeta had witnessed strange things here, but that didn't necessarily mean they'd happened because of Norah.

"You claim to be a dragon goddess,"

Greeta said. "Then prove it. Turn into a dragon. Or create some dragons out of ice. Or do whatever it is you do that makes you a dragon goddess."

Norah roared, spreading her arms out to her side as if they were wings. Her long dark hair flared out like rays from the sun.

Nothing happened.

Norah coughed, and her hair floated back down upon her shoulders. "Too weak."

Erik made a noise as if clearing his throat, even though Frayka had left his throat behind in the castle. "Finehurst did that to her. Murdered all of us with the tapestry he stole, brought us here, and then cast enchantment on us with the tapestry. Kidnapped the dragon goddess and brought her here, too. Cut off strips of it to imprison her. Used the magic inside the tapestry to control her." The flames in his eye sockets flared. "But when people use magic, it's been my experience you can turn their own magic against them. If you know what you're doing."

Norah stared at him. "How?"

Erik grinned, revealing his shard-like

teeth. "Help me get the rest of my body, and I'll tell you how."

"Body," Norah said. "After you tell."

"Fine. The body can come later." Erik cleared his non-existent throat again. "Far as I can tell, using magic seems like using a sword. If someone aims a strike, you counter with a block and then you can follow that with a strike at the person who attacks you." He winked. "And sometimes you catch them by surprise and steal their weapon out of their very hands before they know what's happened."

"No weapon," Norah said, showing her empty hands.

"Ah," Erik said, glancing up at Frayka when she rested his head on the icy ground. "But Finehurst used a weapon again you."

"The tapestry," Greeta and Frayka said in unison.

"Strips from it," Erik said. "And look where they are now."

Everyone looked at the long strip of tapestry that still crawled on the surface of the moat like an indecisive caterpillar.

"And the Northlander girl wrapped another around her sword." Erik's gaze shifted to Greeta. "Call upon the magic in each and you can harness the power you need."

Norah leaned down toward him. "How?" she whispered.

"Call the pieces of tapestry to you. Command the threads binding it together. It's what Finehurst did."

Norah knelt at the edge of the moat, reaching toward the strip crawling on its surface. "Threads of gold and red, bring yourselves to me."

One end of the strip rose like a head turning to look at Norah. It paused as if unsure what to do or where to go.

"Now!" Norah hissed.

The tapestry strip trembled.

Startled by its response, Norah's voice softened. When she spoke, she seemed to be reasoning out what had been done to her. "No fault of yours. Evil man controlled you. He controlled me. Help me. Make things right."

The strip flattened itself against the moat's frozen surface as if trying to hide.

"We can still see you," Erik said to the tapestry strip.

Norah stretched one hand above the

moat, the surface directly beneath her arm melting in response. A tiny crack appeared and a thin flame struggled to emerge. "Your threads honor dragons. Honor me."

The strip of tapestry shuddered and then drew itself upright. It raced across the moat and into Norah's outstretched hand.

Turning toward Greeta, Norah extended her free hand toward the sword. "And you!" Norah cried.

The tapestry strip that Greeta had wrapped around her sword came undone, swirling in the air like a flock of birds in a storm. It whipped into Norah's hands.

Extending a hand toward each woman, Norah commanded the tapestry strips in her hands. "Make them obey me."

One tapestry strip wrapped around Greeta's head, gagging and leashing her like a horse. She saw the other tapestry strip do the same to Frayka. Struggling, Greeta tried to free herself but the tapestry proved to be as strong as iron.

Norah still held onto one end of each strip. She snapped them like reins. "Help me cross."

Although Greeta had quickly realized

she couldn't free herself, Frayka twisted and turned, trying to break loose.

"Don't wear yourself out," Erik advised. "There's nothing you can do but follow orders."

Frayka yelled at him, but the part of the strip gagging her mouth jumbled her words.

Erik rolled to the edge of the moat. "I recommend obeying the goddess's orders and taking her across the moat."

Greeta saw no other option. She took Frayka by the arm and dragged her onto the frozen flames of the moat. When she succeeded in wrangling Frayka by her side, Greeta heard Norah cry out and felt a heavy weight. Twisting her head, Greeta saw that Norah had climbed onto her back and Frayka's back. Norah's slender hand gripped her shoulder.

"Cross!" Norah commanded.

Still clinging to Frayka's arm, Greeta pulled her forward across the moat. The weight on her back lightened and soon she noticed little more than Norah's firm grip on her shoulder. Glancing back, Greeta saw the dragon goddess holding onto their shoulders but her body seemed to float, looking as if it were made of mist instead of flesh and bone. Frightened by the sight, Greeta faced forward again.

It's nothing more than your imagination. It's impossible for anyone to turn into mist. It's impossible to control people with bits of cloth.

Just as impossible to turn ice into dragons, and I fought those dragons. Just as impossible for dead men to make new bodies out of dirt and rocks and plants, but I've met those men. One of them is still with us.

Greeta didn't know what to believe anymore. Nothing like this had ever happened in the Great Turtle Lands. Unless, of course, one counted the fact that Greeta had turned into a dragon without meaning to or knowing how she did it.

For now, she decided to push aside her fear and take one step at a time.

When they reached the opposite side of the moat, Greeta and Frayka climbed onto the opposite bank while Erik's head rolled next to them.

Norah seemed to float down like a cloud descending from the sky. Still holding onto the tapestry reins she said, "Where is Finehurst?" She looked across the landscape as if expecting to see him.

"Finehurst isn't here," Erik said.

Frayka collapsed on the ground at Norah's feet, digging her fingers between the tapestry and her face to no avail.

"What?" Norah said, astonished.

"He trapped you in that ice palace years ago. Then he tricked me and my men into the sand lands where he must have thought no one would ever find us." Erik cast his glance at Greeta and Frayka. "If not for them coming to look for you, we would have been stuck there forever. Before Finehurst left us, he cast a spell that would keep us there until mortals entered our home. That's the only reason we escaped."

"Escaped," Norah repeated, dazed by his words.

The ice beneath their feet rumbled. A roar escaped from the ice castle standing behind them.

Spinning around to look at the ice castle, Greeta saw black cracks run up its walls from the ground. Splitting sounds pierced the air as the castle fell apart.

The last ice dragon rushed out of the ruins on one good foot and one stump.

Pausing at the edge of the moat where fire bubbled once more, it howled mournfully.

Mist crashed like dust from the ruins. Moments later, a man stepped forward through that mist. Greeta recognized him immediately.

Finehurst.

CHAPTER 28

With the moat forming a barrier between them, Finehurst cast a look of disdain toward them.

Norah shrieked at him.

The mist shimmered around Finehurst and made him look ethereal and unworldly. His long blond hair floated in the air like seaweed in water. His pale skin appeared translucent. His fine clothing wafted in a non-existent breeze, seemingly weightless. Without a word, Finehurst raised his arms toward the sky.

The remains of the ice castle hovered above the ground and arranged together in new and unexpected ways. Instead of rising high like a castle, the icy chunks spread out in a long but narrow shape. While it took form, the screams of men filled the air.

Greeta thought she recognized the stones and other bits of Erik's men weave into the strange formation. With a start, she recognized the shape. "It's a ship," she said. "He's creating a ship out of the ruins of the ice castle and Erik's men."

Finehurst pointed at the ice dragon, motioning it toward the ship taking form. Still howling in protest, the ice dragon seemed to be dragged away by invisible hands and forced to form the front of the ship and its icy masthead.

Within moments, the formation took its final shape to look precisely like a Northlander ship. Its large square sail was made of mist. It drifted to rest on the ground long enough for Finehurst to sit on its low rail and swing his legs over to board the ship.

The moment Finehurst climbed aboard, the vessel lifted into the air, sailed above the moat, and landed beyond it on the ice. Its misty sail billowed, and the ship sped away, sliding across the icy ground.

Greeta stared at the vanishing ship, filled with distress. How could she go home now that she'd found Finehurst? How could she ignore the opportunity to stop a man who had already proven his desire to control other people, including the Shining Star people?

I can't go home yet. Finehurst may be here in the Land of Ice now, but what if he returns to the Great Turtle Lands? What if this is my only chance to protect others from him?

Norah pointed at the disappearing ship. "Bad man!" Picking up the ends of the tapestry strips still attached to Greeta and Frayka, Norah attempted to run after Finehurst only to be stopped by the weight of the two women. Frustrated, Norah said, "Too weak." She paused, taking a moment to find her balance. "Need ship."

Nodding toward Frayka, Greeta said, "Her people have ships. And I imagine they'd be happy to share one with a dragon goddess."

"As long as you send no more ice dragons," Frayka said to Norah.

"Ice dragons get attention," Norah said. "Bring you to me."

"Of course," Erik said. "The ice dragons

RESA NELSON

were a call for help. But you made the right assumption all along, Frayka. There was a sorcerer at work. The sorcerer wasn't Norah. The sorcerer was Finehurst. What you didn't know was we'd be facing both a sorcerer *and* a goddess."

Greeta nudged Frayka. "It makes sense. She was trapped inside the ice. It's a wonder she could do anything at all, much less find a way to send ice dragons."

Frayka crossed her arms, standing firm while she faced the goddess. "And we need your protection."

Norah nodded her consent. The goddess pointed anxiously in the direction of the ice ship that had vanished. "Must follow!"

Emboldened, Frayka said, "And plenty of rain so we can grow food. It wouldn't hurt for the sea to drive plenty of fish toward the shore to make them easier to catch."

Norah nodded. "Must go!"

Frayka gestured toward the tapestry strip binding her. "And it wouldn't hurt to set me free."

"Need ship." Norah stared at her for a long moment. "Now!"

A sharp tap against Greeta's leg startled

her. She looked down to see Erik's head.

"Finehurst headed east," Erik said, gesturing with his eyes in the opposite way from which they had come.

"How would you know?" Frayka said.

"When Finehurst brought us here, he sailed around the Land of Ice before landing. This country is an island. A very large island." Erik rolled a few feet away, fixated on the east. "I remember seeing the ice castle from the easternmost point."

"But how can we catch up with Finehurst?" Greeta said. "His ship is too fast."

"We use what we have," Erik said. "He used ice and stone to slide across the glacier surrounding us. We'll do likewise to catch up to him."

Frayka spread her arms, the strip of tapestry dangling from one. "But we have nothing!"

Erik rolled to rest at Norah's feet and looked up at her. "You want to make Finehurst pay for what he did to you? Stop him from ever doing anything like it again?"

"Yes!" Norah hissed.

"Then set the girls free," Erik said. "Because the very thing that Finehurst used to lock you up is what's going to help us catch him."

CHAPTER 29

Following Erik's instruction, Greeta and Frayka placed the tapestry strips that Norah freed from them on the ground. Side by side, the cloth created a place for the three of them to sit, one behind the other. With Greeta at the front, they convinced Norah to sit close behind her.

"Scrunch up, Dragon Goddess," Frayka said. "Or we'll each go flying in different directions if we hit a bump."

Still seething with anger at Finehurst, Norah took the advice despite appearing uncomfortable with it.

"Hold on tight," Erik said while he squeezed between Greeta's feet outstretched at the front ends of the tapestry strips.

"Let me guide." He paused. "Unless I fly off a cliff. If that happens, you take over the steering."

After placing her hands on Norah's back, Frayka pushed and ran. Once the make-shift sled moved enough to gain its own momentum, Frayka hopped onto the tail end of the tapestry strips.

They soon found themselves heading down a glacial route of gentle slopes that led to steeper ones. Greeta clamped her jaw shut tight to keep her teeth from rattling while they plummeted at dizzying speeds. The cold wind in her face numbed her skin. The landscape passing by blurred into vague shapes of white and gray. And the tapestry did little to cushion her body from the bumpy surface of the ice underneath it.

Greeta heard Frayka shouting but the rushing wind drowned out her words. Greeta suspected they might have something to do with the tapering path ahead and what appeared to be a sudden drop.

Despite Erik's earlier suggestion, Greeta noticed any attempt to steer did little good. She could shift their direction slightly by pressing one heel or the other against the tapestry and the ice below, but she'd found no other way to control their journey. Now that their path narrowed abruptly, Greeta clenched her teeth, knowing the best she could do was hope they wouldn't sail over the edge and plummet to their deaths.

At the sound of Norah's muffled voice behind her back, Greeta remembered they had the good grace to have a dragon goddess with them.

Seemingly in response to Norah's voice, a small overhead cloud burst into a snow squall. Illuminated by the sun, the snow flakes surrounding them sparkled bright and reflected the sun's rays at new angles that revealed grooves in the path.

The grooves are the marks left by Finehurst's ship when it slid down this path. All we have to do is stay within them. They'll keep us on track and safe!

Understanding the importance of what she saw, Greeta dug one heel against the tapestry and shifted direction just enough for them to fall into one of those grooves, which curved safely around the sharp bend ahead and kept them on track.

The hills became even steeper, causing

them to slide along the twisting and turning path at breakneck speeds. But once inside the grooves left by Finehurst's ship, Greeta had no problem keeping them on course. Eventually, the path leveled off and allowed them to come to a gradual stop where they could stand and walk.

Once off the glacier, they came upon a wide path of black sand that led down to the east shore. Erik rolled ahead of them, skidding to a stop every so often to wait for them to catch up.

The black path opened upon a rocky beach where waves crashed, booming like thunderstorms. Dark clouds crowded the sky, and the dim light made it easier to hear the ocean than to see it.

Greeta scanned the horizon but saw no sign of the ship or Finehurst. The thought that she had noticed something wrong with him nagged at her.

Norah ran into the sea. She stopped knee-deep, howling and sinking until the water reached her shoulders.

Greeta stood next to Frayka. "What is Norah doing?"

A wave crashed over the goddess's head, making it look like Norah had disappeared. But moments later she stood, looking stronger and radiant.

"Nourishing herself," Erik said. "Becoming whole in a way she hasn't been since Finehurst imprisoned her." He sighed, and his fiery eyes dimmed until they looked like glowing embers of a dying fire.

Striding out of the ocean, Norah stood tall and renewed. With the snap of her fingers, she commanded the tapestry strips to wrap around each of her own hands.

Erik rolled back to make eye contact with her. "Better?"

Norah deigned to look into his fiery eyes for a moment instead of answering. She pointed toward the south. "Ship."

Following where Norah pointed, Greeta saw nothing. But she believed the dragon goddess knew where to find Finehurst.

CHAPTER 30

Moving down the beach quickly and around a bend, they spotted a long wooden ship beached ahead on the black sand shore. However, it looked like a Northlander vessel made by mortal hands instead of the strange one fashioned from ice and dead men by Finehurst.

Norah squinted into the distance as if it improved her sight. "Fine ship. Many gone. One remains."

"What is that supposed to mean?" Frayka muttered, hiking up the muddy hem of her skirt before stepping over a pile of black rocks riddled with holes that blocked her path.

"I'll find out," Erik said. Propelling himself up onto a small dune, he gained enough momentum to roll at a good clip down the beach toward the ship.

"Come," Norah said. "Be ready."

They walked toward the wooden Northlander ship. Greeta made out a figure moving close to it. "Who is that?" she said. When she stopped, the others paused by her side.

Soon the figure in the distance ahead looked up at them and became still.

"One of ours?" Frayka said, her voice laced with hope.

The figure raced toward them, fine black sand spraying outward with every running footstep.

Within moments Greeta recognized him from Blackstone. "It's Njall."

The sea split apart and Finehurst's gleaming ship of ice rose from its depths, draped in seaweed. It sped from water onto land, skidding and cutting a path between Njall and the Northlander women.

Finehurst leapt over the far railing of his ship, disappearing from sight.

"Njall!" Frayka cried out, running toward the ship.

Greeta stood still, worried because the

ice ship blocked her view of Finehurst and Njall.

Moments later, she saw Finehurst climb back aboard his ice ship. He hauled Njall onboard, bound and gagged by seaweed. Finehurst pushed Njall down to the deck and then turned to stare at Greeta in defiance.

Something is wrong. What am I not understanding?

"Finehurst!" Norah yelled.

Frayka screamed in anger while she raced toward the ice ship. But before she could reach it, the ship's square sail made of mist billowed. An unusually strong wind filled the strange sail and pushed the ice ship back into the ocean.

"Ship!" Norah called out. She pointed to the wooden Northlander ship from which Njall had come. "Follow him!"

Frayka dug her heels into the sand to stop. She spun toward Norah and stood with the strength of new understanding. Changing direction, Frayka bolted toward the Northlander ship resting on the edge of the beach.

Erik rolled in the same direction. He called to Greeta, "Keep up!"

Greeta sprinted to catch up. She reached the Northlander ship soon after Norah and Frayka climbed aboard. Greeta leaned down and scooped Erik's head in her arms before hopping over the low rail and onto the deck. Running to the center of the ship, Greeta then raised the sail, grateful when Frayka helped her.

Norah raised her gaze to the sky above. "Help me!"

Thunder rumbled as if to answer, and the winds filled the sail just as the Northlander women finished raising it.

The winds jerked the ship out to sea until it followed the path of Finehurst's ice ship. Greeta and Frayka scurried to secure the oars, lying in a pile below the sail.

Norah glided to the front of the ship where she stood behind its figurehead, carved in the shape of a dragon's head. She stood as still as wood and kept her gaze fixed on the ice ship skimming through the waters ahead.

Greeta watched the shore of the Land of Ice grow distant. When it disappeared from sight, night fell and Greeta sat on the deck with the intent of resting her eyes for just a moment.

But she soon fell victim to the exhaust-tion of the day she'd survived.

CHAPTER 31

The next thing she knew, Greeta realized she had crossed over into the Dreamtime.

She found herself walking between her mother Astrid and friend Margreet in a familiar village made up of odd-looking houses nestled into the ground, a lively blacksmithing station, and a more private one a short distance away near the edge of the sea.

"So you have met the most peculiar Norah," Margreet said.

"She isn't peculiar," Astrid protested. "She endured horrible things, and those things changed her."

Margreet cast a glance of admiration and sympathy at Astrid. "You endured them, too."

Distressed, Greeta turned to the mother she had never met in real life, only here in the Dreamtime. "What horrible things?"

"Things that happened because of my family," Astrid said, her voice soft and distant. "Decisions they made. Nothing you need worry about."

"Why are you keeping secrets from me?" Greeta said, her distress growing by the moment. "Papa and Auntie Peppa keep secrets from me, too. I need to know. If you leave me in the dark, I could get hurt because of what I don't know."

"Your child speaks true," Margreet said. Her body dissolved into mist and blew away with the wind.

Greeta didn't mind. She knew that whenever she walked in the Dreamtime, very strange things were likely to happen. Looking at Astrid, she said, "Mama, please. There is a Northlander man. Finehurst. I believe he is on the verge of hurting a great many people."

"I know Finehurst. I met him long ago."

Astrid's response left Greeta speechless.

"You are right to suspect him of terrible things to come," Astrid said. "I have an idea. Follow me."

They walked past the blacksmiths at work amidst trenches of fire, barrels of quenching water, rows of tools laid out on benches, and a dozen anvils. The sound of iron ringing against iron filled the air, and the smoke from the fires made Greeta's nose twitch.

Passing a few houses, they walked from the edge of the village along a narrow spit of land toward Astrid's cottage and private smithery.

"I believe it should be somewhere here," Astrid said. She sat on the ground at the side of her cottage and began digging between the bright yellow flowers growing alongside her home.

Greeta knelt beside her. "What are you looking for?"

"Everything happening now is because of what happened in the past," Astrid said. "Long before you came into being."

Desperate, Greeta said, "Tell me. Please."

The scent of newly-turned earth filled the air with promise.

"I knew Norah twice in my life," Astrid said, continuing to dig. "In my final days and in my early days. My beginning and my end times. In the early days, we were both used by my family. They did shocking things, but I think their intent was good." Astrid shook her head, her face sagging in disappointment. "They didn't think ahead to imagine what the consequences might be."

Greeta brightened. "Like the seven generations!"

Astrid hesitated, staring at Greeta. "The what?"

Encouraged, Greeta spoke excitedly. "The people of the Shining Star nation hold one principle dear: they ask themselves how any decision will affect the next seven generations before making that decision. It doesn't matter what kind of decision it is. It can be large or small. Uncle Killing Crow taught me. He showed me how to put myself in the shoes of others and consider their feelings before I say or do anything."

Mystified, Astrid sat back, pulling her empty hands out of the ground. "The demons taught you that?"

"Demons?"

"I know someone whose grandmother

told him our people crossed the Western Sea long ago and discovered the Land of Vines. But the Northlanders abandoned any hope of settling there because of the demons."

Aghast to hear the story again, Greeta could only manage to say, "What?"

"Screeching demons. Creatures with wings in their hair and painted faces. Monsters armed with sharp stone daggers and ax blades. They're said to scream horribly when they cut off men's heads."

Taking her mother's words as a personal insult, Greeta said, "Some of us wear feathers in our hair. And men paint their faces when they must go to war to protect us from others who attack. But we are not monsters and there is no beheading of any kind." Greeta paused, reconsidering her words. "I wouldn't call it screaming, but when we defend ourselves there can be a lot of shouting."

Astrid chose a new spot to dig. "That's not what Lumpy told me. His grandmother had a talent for portents, but this wasn't any kind of prediction. It really happened. And you know the Northlanders. No one scares us." She shuddered. "Except for those screeching demons Lumpy's grand-mother told him about."

"Lumpy," Greeta repeated, thinking back to when she had first been abducted from her Shining Star village in the Great Turtle Lands. Her first impression of the two Northlanders who confronted her was that one looked as if his nose had been broken and the other had a lumpy fore-head. "Are you talking about Thorkel?"

Astrid scrunched up her nose. "Thor-kel? Can't remember meeting anyone by that name."

Greeta described his appearance and then said, "I first met him months ago when he and his friend with the broken nose took me on their ship and I found out they knew Papa. Thorkel's grandmother came from the Far East, and she had a ta-lent for portents, like you said."

"That must be them," Astrid said, laughing. "The next time you see Lumpy and Broken Nose, ask them how they came to look the way they do today."

Anxious to get answers, Greeta made another attempt. "That's all fine, but you're not telling me what I want to know. Norah called me a Scalding. Is that your family name? Are those the people who hurt you? And what does this have to do with Finehurst?"

"Before you can understand Finehurst, you must understand Norah and the past I share with her." Removing her hands from the dirt once more, Astrid shifted closer to Greeta in order to dig in a new spot between the yellow flowers. "Yes. Scalding is my family name."

Taking her mother's advice, Greeta focused on learning about the past. "Frayka sang a children's rhyme about the Scaldings. It says things about dragons. And about how dangerous the Scaldings are. That they lock people up in towers. And there are dragons. Did they put dragons in towers with people?"

"Here it is!" Astrid beamed. Working her fingers into the ground, she pulled out a handful of earth. First she shook the dirt away from what she held, brushed more away with her fingers, and then rubbed it against her clothing. Astrid placed several flower roots in the center of her hand and showed them to Greeta.

The roots looked white and almost transparent. In Astrid's hand they changed to a metallic color, twisting and bending around each other until they formed something beautiful.

"This is what a silver brooch I once owned looked like," Astrid said. "It is the most important gift anyone ever gave to me, because it saved my life."

CHAPTER 32

Greeta stared at the silver brooch, as big as the palm of Astrid's hand. The flower roots Astrid pulled from the ground turned into several strands of silver that wove together, forming two snakes encircling a dragon, long and serpentine.

"When my family gave me to a childseller," Astrid said, "I recognized the danger. A seller can keep each child for only so long before the responsibility of feeding the child outweighs the seller's potential profit. Sellers either let go of or kill any child that doesn't sell within a week or so."

Horrified, Greeta could only stare silently at her mother.

Astrid smiled. "But then I met a dragonslayer and his son, who gave this brooch to me. It's a special brooch. They told me to show it to the local blacksmith as a signal he would recognize. A signal that he should buy me and teach me his trade. That's how I became a blacksmith."

Finally finding her voice, Greeta said, "Your family gave you away?"

Ignoring her, Astrid continued. "I needed help. This brooch changed my life. The dragonslayers and the blacksmith saved me." She closed her fingers around the brooch and when she opened her hand again, the silver brooch had changed back to flower roots. She let them fall to the ground. "And later I used it to save another's life."

"But your family," Greeta said, overwhelmed by everything her mother had told her. "They gave you away. How can anyone do that to their own child? How can anyone do something so evil?"

"The world is not such a simple place." Astrid's eyes darkened. "I told you the Scaldings had good intent. Sometimes good people unwittingly do bad things with good intentions. Sometimes bad people unwittingly do good things with bad intentions."

The sudden darkening in her mother's eyes gave Greeta pause. She wondered how such evil had affected her.

Astrid's expression softened. "Did your father teach you about the character of iron?"

Greeta thought back to the day and night in Blackstone when she helped Papa forge the sword she still carried at her side. "Yes. He said each bloom of iron has its own character: either weak or strong."

"Good." Astrid smiled. "And why does that matter when you make a dragonslayer's sword?"

"You hammer each bloom into a billet, so each billet is either weak or strong. Then you twist several billets together to make a sword because they're likely to be both strong and weak, which makes the sword strong but flexible."

Astrid's smile broadened. "And can you tell the character of a sword by looking at it?"

"No. There's nothing about the appearance of a bloom of iron or a sword that tells you if its character is weak or strong. The only way you find out is by using it."

Astrid tilted her head to one side as if to take a closer look in Greeta's eyes. "And what causes you to use a sword?"

Greeta hesitated. "Mostly to defend oneself, I suppose."

"I know you miss your home and your everyday life," Astrid said. "But consider this: people are like swords. When life is peaceful and good, you have no way of knowing what anyone's true character is. It's strife that puts people to the test and reveals who they really are." She leaned forward and let her voice drop to a whisper. "You're being tested, and that's a good thing."

Startled, Greeta stared at her mother. "What if I don't want...?"

"Never mind," Astrid said. She leaned back and spoke in a normal tone. "I showed the brooch to you because a simple thing like that changed my life forever. It made all the good things that followed possible. I believe all Norah wants is someone who can give her the help she needs."

"She took me captive. I have to get free so I can stop Finehurst."

"You can stop Finehurst by helping Norah," Astrid said. "She truly is a goddess."

"But how do I help a dragon goddess?"

Astrid pushed the flower roots she'd pulled up back into the dirt, pushing everything back in place. "Be there for her. Just be there."

Thunder clapped above. But when Greeta looked up, she saw a clear blue sky.

Frayka's voice filled the air. "Hey, wake up!"

In the blink of an eye, Greeta found herself on board the ship, still at sea. The village and her mother and the Dreamtime had vanished. Greeta struggled to come fully awake, finding herself curled up on the deck floor.

The tapestry strips once again bound her and Frayka to Norah like ponies to a cart.

Standing, Greeta saw the ice ship ahead in the distance. A great swelling sea surrounded the wooden Northlander ship, which navigated successfully between each swell. Waves climbed as high as towering trees and filled the air with spray that drenched like rain. Her lips tasted like salt, and her throat felt parched.

After a few days of dangerous waves, the sea became calmer although dark clouds crowded the skies again.

"Look," Frayka said, pointing over the ship's railing. "Finehurst's ship went there."

Rising to her feet, Greeta saw no land. Instead, she stared at waves of golden light dancing upon the sea surrounding their own Northlander ship.

She saw Finehurst's ice ship sinking into the golden light that filled the water below.

CHAPTER 33

"Njall!" Frayka cried, pointing at the sinking ice ship. "Finehurst still has him!"

She climbed on the rail, ready to dive in even though the tapestry keeping her bound to Norah wouldn't allow it.

"Wait!" Greeta cried, pointing toward the water. A figure in its depths struggled toward the surface.

The light dancing upon the sea illuminated not only the surface of the sea but its depths as well. It was as if the sun had fallen into the sea and spread its light throughout its deep waters.

Frayka stepped back down on the deck. "Is it Finehurst?"

Moments later, the figure broke through

the surface, gasping for air.

"Njall!" Frayka cried. Reaching over the rail, she hauled him on board.

"Why did Finehurst let you go?" Greeta said.

Njall coughed and struggled to breathe, unable to answer.

Frayka knelt by him and removed all that bound and gagged him.

Greeta watched Finehurst's ice ship sink through the light toward a cracked, gleaming tower suspended in the water a short distance below, and it seemed to be the source of the light. The tower's golden surface caught and reflected beams of light and cast them in all directions. Piles of rubble hung suspended around it as if some kind of magic prevented everything from sinking to the ocean floor far below. At what appeared to be the top of the tower, Greeta saw something stretching away, something solid and still.

Frayka said, "I think I know what that is. But I don't know why Finehurst would come here unless he knows about you."

But before Frayka could say another word, Norah climbed on top of the ship's rail alongside them. Holding on tight to the tapestry reins that bound the women to her, Norah plunged into the sea, taking Greeta and Frayka with her.

The hard surface of the water slammed into Greeta's face and stunned her for a moment. The reality of drowning pushed her into a state of terror. Next to her, Frayka cried out underwater, her words unintelligible. Frayka wriggled in protest, but she accomplished nothing more than knotting the tapestry rein tighter around herself.

Although the water blurred Greeta's vision, the bright light cast from the tower made it easy to see a school of silver fish darting past. Sinking deeper, Greeta felt the pain of changing pressure in her ears. Struggling to keep holding her breath and fighting the need to gasp for air, she felt like a rock sinking too fast.

Looking down, she saw Norah undulating like a dolphin, dragging them toward the gleaming tower.

Why are we going toward the tower instead of Finehurst's ship?

Nearing the tower, Greeta understood the image she'd seen reaching from its top. This close, she could make out its shape clearly. Greeta saw an image made of iron: a woman holding a sword high above her head.

Feeling weak, Greeta looked up at the surface of the sea. The last thing she saw was the bottom of the wooden Northlander ship where Njall and Eric remained, growing more distant by the moment.

*　*　*

When Greeta awoke, she found herself lying next to Frayka in the middle of a spiral stairway whose stone steps stretched far above and below them. Although the tapestry reins still bound the Northlander women, Norah had vanished.

Groggy, Greeta sat up. As she did so, her perspective of the world changed. The ceiling above her head turned out to be the side of the tower. And the spiral stairway no longer stretched above and below but to her right and left instead.

"The tower," Greeta said, remembering what she'd seen before Norah had pulled her into the ocean. "It tilts on its side." The panic of being submerged under water struck her like a slap to the head until she realized only a small amount of water covered the area below her feet and that it didn't seem she'd need to worry about drowning any time soon. But her clothes were drenched and cold against her skin, making her shiver.

She turned her attention to Frayka, even more tangled in the tapestry strip bound around her. Greeta shook her shoulder. "Frayka. Wake up."

Frayka coughed, spitting out a mouthful of water. Still coughing, she sat up next to Greeta. "What happened?"

"Norah brought us into the ocean and inside this place. You said you recognize it. Where are we?"

Staring in all directions, Frayka said, "I think this is Tower Island, but I'm not sure. The place I heard of was an island with a tall golden tower. How could it be underwater?" The same moment of panic hit Frayka. "And why aren't we drowning?"

"I don't know. Maybe its doors were sealed when it sank. What matters is that we have air to breathe."

Still knotted up, Frayka squirmed. "I have to get out. And what about Finehurst? We saw his ship sink. Did he drown?"

"I don't know. But I think Finehurst's

ship must have sunk to the bottom. Be still." Greeta examined the way the tapestry strip had tangled up around Frayka and then worked slowly and methodically to work those tangles loose. "We didn't sink terribly far. It's not like we're on the bottom of the sea."

"How does that any sense?" Frayka said, holding herself still and watching Greeta. "We should be on the bottom of the sea. This place should be on the bottom of the sea."

Greeta smiled. "How does it make sense that ice dragons attacked your settlement? Or that we met dead men who became our friends?"

"They're not our friends," Frayka said. "And there's a simple explanation. We thought the ice dragons had to come from sorcery but it turned out to be the workings of a dragon goddess, not a sorcerer. Although the dead men exist because of Finehurst and the sorcery he seems to have learned."

Greeta paused and gestured to their surroundings. "And how is this any different from what we've already experienced?"

Frayka stared at her for a long moment.

"Don't you know?"

Still working the tangles loose, Greeta shook her head.

"Don't you remember the rhyme?" Frayka said. "Tower Island?"

Greeta remembered.

Mind yourself
Mind your thoughts
Or Scaldings
Tie you into knots

That memory instead of her cold, wet clothes made her shiver.

Frayka gazed at her steadily. "Tower Island is the home of the Scaldings. This would have been your family home if any other Scaldings still lived."

Fear crept up on Greeta. She remembered what her mother had told her in the Dreamtime. Tower Island was where her mother's own family had caged her with a dragon. "Bad things happened here."

"Yes," Frayka said. "Bad things happened."

Inside the far end of the tower, they heard Norah calling.

CHAPTER 34

"Taddeo!" Norah called, her voice echoing throughout the length of the toppled tower. Within moments, she came into sight, making her way over the winding steps that wrapped above and around Norah because the tower lay sideways. She looked as if she were walking through the mouth of a sea serpent whose teeth spiraled all the way down to its stomach.

"We have to get out," Frayka said. "Who knows why she brought us here or what she wants? We have to get away from her. Dragon gods are unpredictable."

In answer, Greeta held up the end of the tapestry rein that she had finally untangled from Frayka, still attached but no longer knotted and twisted around her legs. "We're still bound to her. She may have left us here, but we can't get away."

Whispering, Frayka said, "We don't know that unless we try to escape!"

Approaching them, Norah focused on the shallow water lining the length of the tower. Looking into it, she shouted, "Taddeo!"

"We have to try!" Frayka insisted.

"You!" Norah pointed at Greeta and marched up to her. "All your fault!"

Irritated, Greeta stood squarely to face her. "I have done nothing but offer to help you. Why are you blaming me?" She gestured to the empty tower surrounding them. "And what are you blaming me for?"

"Scalding!" Norah said, infuriated. "Destroy all!"

"Norah, enough," a disembodied male voice said, echoing all around them.

"Taddeo?" Brightening, Norah turned and spoke with hope. "Uncle Taddeo?"

The shallow water rose up as mist, forming the shape of a man, transparent and yet visible. "What happened to you, child?"

Norah jabbed an accusing finger at

Greeta. "Scalding!"

The mist transformed its shape into that of a dragon, and it stepped toward them until its wet nose nuzzled Greeta's hair, inhaling like a sharp winter wind. "Truly a Scalding." The mist dragon took a step back, looking from Greeta to Norah. "One survives. But not one I knew. This one is recent and new." When the mist dragon sighed, fog poured from its mouth. "You cannot blame the Scaldings for everything that goes wrong. What happened, Norah?"

Frayka tugged at Greeta's elbow and gestured toward one end of the tower as if suggesting they make a run for it.

Greeta shook her head. Clearly, Taddeo had to be Norah's family. He had not only come to Greeta's defense but encouraged Norah to tell her story. Instinctively, Greeta believed she needed to hear and understand the details. Her mother had encouraged Greeta to help Norah, and any information she could glean now was bound to help.

"Tell me who did this to you," the mist dragon said.

Norah's voice became flat and distant.

"Mortal man. Finehurst. Found me."

The mist dragon sank to its belly and rested its chin on its forepaws. "And then?"

Norah reached toward the women and picked up the ends of the tapestry strips she used to control them. "Used this. Forced me back into this world." Her voice strained with grief. "This horrible world."

"It's not that bad," Frayka muttered.

"Maybe it is for her," Greeta whispered.

"Let me see," the mist dragon said.

Norah tugged on the tapestry strips, forcing Greeta and Frayka to come several steps forward. Norah then held the ends in her hand, showing them to the creature.

He poked at the fabric with his nose, leaving damp spots on it.

A few loose threads wriggled out of the frayed edges of the strip where it had been torn from the tapestry that had once been intact. One gold thread, one silver, and one bright red. Each gleamed with the same intensity as the exterior of the tower when Greeta had first seen it shining underwater.

The mist dragon flicked its watery tongue and touched each thread with it.

He then said, "Release the women and show me each piece of this tapestry laid out to show its full length."

"No!" Norah said. "Need them!"

The mist dragon turned to look at Greeta. "Scalding girl. Have you not already committed to helping my niece?"

Greeta looked at the creature in fright. She had indeed promised to help Norah, but the only place that had happened was in the Dreamtime. Greeta had mentioned it to no one. How could this creature know Greeta's experience in the Dreamtime?

Too troubled by this thought to speak, Greeta simply nodded.

Turning back to Norah, the mist dragon said, "I must study the fabric before I can understand it in full. Until then, I will not know how to help you."

Norah stood still and silent, seeming to absorb the creature's conditions. Without another word, she gathered up the end of each tapestry rein in her hand and with one mighty jerk, snapped them free and away from Greeta and Frayka.

"Each of you," the mist dragon said to the women, "spread out your piece of the tapestry across the steps so I can see from one end to the other."

Frayka obeyed immediately, looking relieved but apprehensive at her unexpected freedom.

Greeta followed, laying out the strip of tapestry that had bound her to Norah beneath Frayka's cloth. She climbed over the angular steps beneath her feet to the tower wall surface on the opposite side of the stairs, where she stood with Frayka.

The mist dragon paced along the smooth interior wall of the tilted tower, its watery talons plopping against the stone surface like raindrops against leaves. Hoisting itself onto the steps with its front paws, the mist dragon examined each tapestry strip and the loose threads carefully. "This is a family tapestry," he said. "One created to record the history of a family other than Scaldings. A Southlander family. Its past generations. Important things accomplished by family members. And events of the times in which they lived."

"Mortals?" Norah said.

"Mostly," the mist dragon said. "But they knew dragons. Our kind, not the other."

Other? Does he mean the dragons that act like dangerous animals instead of gods?

The mist dragon continued. "I see evidence they worked with dragons. Perhaps some we know." He paused at the edge of Greeta's strip, nosing the partial image of a dragon's leg. "Perhaps even me."

"Finehurst used it," Norah said. "He locked me away."

The mist dragon took his time circling the tapestry strips, continuing to study them. "He discovered a way to unlock the tapestry's power. Only then can one tear such a treasure apart. Once in pieces, it can be used against anyone and anything related to its images."

"Not me!" Norah protested. Pointing at the tapestry strips, she said, "Where am I on there?"

Looking at Greeta, the mist dragon said, "Switch the pieces."

With Frayka's help, Greeta picked up one strip and moved it above the other.

The loose threads along the ragged bottom of one strip wriggled and reached out toward the threads along the top of the strip beneath it. Similar colors from each

302

piece found and encircled each other until they bonded. The threads tightened, closing the distance between each strip until they edged against each other. The seam between them vanished, and the two strips merged into a single piece.

Norah wrapped her arms around herself and shivered. Her back straightened, and she stood taller.

"Better?" the mist dragon said.

"Better." Norah nodded. She moved her arms in wide circles. "More free."

Nosing the newly assembled strips, the mist dragon gestured at the image of a dragon rising out of the ocean. "Here we are. The mortal chose to tear off this part of the tapestry with us in mind. That is why he could control you."

"I told you she's a water dragon!" Frayka whispered to Greeta.

The mist dragon snapped his head toward Frayka. "And you are a Far East girl." Stepping over the tapestry piece toward her, he sniffed at Frayka's hair. "Not all Far East blood but enough to matter. I also come from the Far East."

"My great-grandmother," Frayka stammered. "I look like her."

Nodding with satisfaction, the mist dragon turned his attention back to Norah. "The only way you can protect yourself and prevent this man from gaining control over you again is to gather all the remaining pieces of this tapestry and reunite them. Once whole, keep the tapestry in a safe place where no mortal can find it. And be sure to ask the young Scalding and the Far East girl for help." With that, the mist dragon faded and disappeared.

"Uncle!" Norah cried out in disappointment. "Why?"

The mist dragon's voice echoed inside the tower. "Because they are more than mere mortals."

CHAPTER 35

"Like I said before," Greeta said to Norah, "we can accomplish more by working together than by working apart."

Norah glared at Greeta and then marched down one length of the tilted tower. "Come!"

Frayka shrugged. "I think she wants us to follow her."

Greeta gathered the single piece of tapestry up in her arms, now larger since the two strips had woven themselves back together, and trailed after Frayka and Norah.

At what appeared to be the base of the tower, Norah gestured to Greeta. "Here!"

Not knowing what else to do, Greeta approached her.

Norah took one end of the tapestry from Greeta and wrapped it around her own wrist. "Hold on." Shifting her gaze to Frayka, Norah said, "Both." She then turned her attention to the closed door to the tower, now above them due to the tower's tilt.

Greeta wrapped the middle section of the tapestry around her arm and gave the rest to Frayka.

Norah reached up to open the door, which fell inward, followed by a rush of water.

Before she could fathom what was happening, Greeta felt herself yanked upwards and held on tightly to the tapestry. Holding her breath, she squeezed her eyes shut, feeling the pressure in her ears shift again. Even though she kept her lips pressed together, she could taste the salt from the sea inside her mouth.

Just as Greeta began to feel light-headed, she broke through the water's surface. Frayka popped up soon after.

The wooden Northlander ship bobbed in the water a short distance away.

Still gripping her end of the tapestry, Norah glided through the gentle waves, pulling Greeta and Frayka behind her.

Njall reached down over the ship's railing and helped them all climb back on board. "What happened? I didn't know what to do."

Ignoring everyone else, Njall hurled himself at Frayka, wrapping his arms around her. "All those months ago when the ice dragons attacked and you rushed after them, I worried about you." Releasing Frayka, Njall held her shoulders and looked into her eyes. "When the chasm appeared, its force knocked our ships out to sea. It took days to retrieve them. We then sailed from our beach to another to make our way around the chasm. We searched inland. We sailed the coasts and looked everywhere for you. The day you found me, I'd stayed behind with the ship while everyone else went inland to search. I wondered if you were lost forever."

A memory struck Greeta, and she felt the need to defend her companion. "I seem to remember you ridiculing her. Didn't you call her Frayka the freak?"

"That was before she proved herself to be the perfect woman." Njall glanced at Greeta as if she were an annoying insect buzzing at his ears. "Didn't you see the way she fought seven ice dragons and killed them all?"

"Seven?" Greeta protested, incensed by his exaggeration. "There were only three ice dragons. And she didn't kill them all herself. She killed one, I killed another, and the last one got away."

Njall stared at Frayka in wonder. "No one believed your portents, except for your father. They seemed so wild and strange. But everything you told us came true."

Greeta recalled the way Frayka often snorted when disgusted, and Greeta snorted in the same way. "*Now* you believe her. But I repeat: I heard you call her Frayka the freak."

Keeping his gaze on Frayka, Njall said, "Any sensible Northlander requires proof before believing in the unproven."

Unfazed by Njall's attention, Frayka turned toward Greeta. "It's true. My talent for portents comes from my great-grandmother. She came from the Far East. No Northlander has ever been able to do what I do." She patted one of Njall's hands before pushing it aside. "Northlanders do have to see to believe. It's how they are."

Njall embraced Frayka again, whose arms splayed awkwardly to either side instead of returning his embrace. She reminded Greeta of a resistant sheep that would rather be grazing on the sod roof of her father's house.

Greeta heard a clattering on the steps leading to the deck below and saw Erik roll up the last step and toward them.

Erik rolled up next to Njall's feet and looked up. "Who do we have here?"

Njall looked down and squealed at the sight of Erik's disembodied head and fiery eyes. Shaking in fright, Njall kicked Erik across the deck. "What was that?" he shrieked.

"Our friend," Greeta said. "Erik, are you all right?"

"Fine," he replied. "Head's in one piece."

Frayka gave Njall a disapproving look. "What a dreadful thing to do. How would you like it if someone gave you a kick in the head without being provoked?"

The color fell from Njall's face. "But it's a monster! A demon's head!"

"I heard that," Erik called out from the opposite side of the deck. "And I don't appreciate the name calling."

Frayka added, "Calling Erik our friend may be stretching the truth a bit, but he has been useful at times. He still might be."

"I can still hear you." Erik finally rolled toward them.

Greeta noticed the rock forming his forehead had cracked. Kneeling, she looked into his eyes, now little more than glowing embers, and said, "Are you all right?"

"Worse for the unexpected assault," Erik said. "But mostly intact."

"Enough, enough, enough!" Norah said. "Sail! Now!"

"But what about Finehurst?" Greeta said. She leaned over the rail and looked into the sea. But the bright golden light gleaming from the tower made it difficult to peer into the depths below. Greeta saw no evidence of his ice ship.

Erik's eyes became brighter. Looking up at Greeta, he said, "There's no use arguing with the dragon goddess." He tilted his head toward Norah. "I think you're right. We can get more done working with each other than fighting against each other."

Greeta sighed at the inconvenience of her own words coming back to haunt her.

Frayka leaned over the rail, wringing the seawater out of her wet clothes. "But you decided to stay here."

Erik rolled up to greet them. Grinning, he said, "That question was still under debate."

"Back to castle," Norah said.

The ice castle is gone. Finehurst destroyed it.

Perplexed, Njall said, "Why?"

Still wringing her skirt, Frayka said, "Because she needs all the pieces torn from the original tapestry so she can put it back together."

"But Finehurst has the rest of the tapestry!" Greeta said. She leaned over the rail and pointed at the sea below. "We have to get it back from him!"

"Just because Finehurst is here doesn't mean the tapestry is here," Frayka said. "It could be anywhere."

Greeta realized Frayka spoke the truth. Greeta had seen the tapestry in Finehurst's mansion in the Great Turtle Lands. It might still be there. Or he might have brought it back to the Land of Ice. It might be in his hands or it might be hidden somewhere.

"The dragon goddess used two strips that imprisoned her to do the same to me and Greeta," Frayka continued. "But there were three strips. It makes more sense to get that third strip right now. She thinks it is still back at her castle."

Surprised, Greeta turned to face Frayka. "It's not?"

Grinning, Frayka said, "Cough it up, Erik."

First, Erik rolled upside down and side to side. With great, hacking coughs, he opened his mouth wide and spit out a tightly rolled strip of cloth.

Shrieking with delight, Norah raced to scoop it up and unroll it. "Other!" she shouted.

Turning to Greeta, Frayka said, "I hated the thought of leaving such a pretty thing behind at the ice castle. When I went back inside and picked up Erik, I jammed it in his mouth. I thought it might come in handy."

Greeta squeezed out water from the tapestry to which she and Frayka had clung and then laid it flat on the deck.

Now that she could get a better look at it, Greeta studied the images.

A handful of fanciful creatures snarled behind men who had dark hair and darker skin than Northlanders, although they looked nothing like the Shining Star people. About the size of horses, the strange creatures looked like colorful snakes with long legs and wings. "What are those supposed to be?"

"Dragons," Erik said. "But they don't look like true dragons. Look how small and delicate they are. Not to mention that real dragons don't have wings. I suppose whoever made the tapestry never saw dragons up close. Maybe all they had to go on was rumors."

Norah placed the cloth that Erik had spit up next to it, shaking bits of dirt from it and her fingers. She took a step back and studied the two pieces of tapestry.

Doing likewise, Greeta saw no way for them to fit together at first. But within moments she noticed something peculiar about an image on the strip that Erik had swallowed. It looked like part of a dragon's body, but only when she tilted her head sideways.

"I think he tore the first two strips from the bottom of the tapestry," Greeta said, stepping forward and picking up one end of the new strip so she could drag it into a new position. "It looks like he might have taken this one from the side."

Greeta repositioned the strip from being parallel to the merged pieces so that it was perpendicular to them. She dragged it until the bottom part of the new strip lined up with the merged pieces.

Once again, threads of all colors loosened and emerged from both pieces, seeking each other out and twisting until the pieces of the tapestry wove themselves together.

Erik struggled to stay in one place while the deck tilted with the waves. "I was there when Finehurst ripped this thing apart. Came from a wealthy man's home. From what I remember, Finehurst might have left some behind."

"On purpose?" Greeta said. "You think he knew someone could stop him by putting the tapestry back together?"

"So he left a piece behind to make it more difficult," Frayka said, nodding her head in agreement.

"Possibly," Erik said. "Most likely, probably."

Norah's face became grim with determination. "Where?"

"A mansion in the Southlands," Erik said.

"The Southlands!" Njall protested. "That's weeks away. And with winter coming soon, it's too dangerous to sail. The seas will be too stormy." He looked to Frayka for confirmation. "No one sails during winter!"

Frayka nodded. "He's right. We should go home and wait for spring."

"No," Norah said quietly. "Now."

"There's another way," Erik said. "We can get there in days, not weeks. All we have to do is sail east until we reach the Northlands coast. I know how to travel from the Northlands to the Midlands and then to the Southlands by river. Instead of having to travel around these countries, we can sail right through them."

Greeta looked into the water below. "What about Finehurst?"

"Gone," Norah said resolutely. "Dead."

Doubt nagged at Greeta, and she wondered if Norah spoke the truth or had made an assumption.

CHAPTER 36

True to Erik's word, they arrived at a port city in the Southlands a few days later. Like all cities in the Southlands, Midlands, and Northlands, this one stood empty and abandoned. No one wanted to rebuild in countries that had been destroyed by dragon gods.

After securing the ship to a weathered post, they followed Erik's direction and travelled by foot until they reached another abandoned town.

"This is Bellesguarde," Erik said, rolling in front of them to lead the way to the edge of town. Simple stone houses jammed against each other, creating narrow city streets made of cobblestones.

A stone manor stood in the distance on a hill. Rising three stories, the building's narrow width made it seem smaller than its true size. A slim tower stretched six stories high on the left side. An enormous iron flower adorned the top of the tower, making the manor look like a gigantic toad shooting its tongue skyward to catch a blossom floating on the breeze. A few sheep grazed on the grassy lawn surrounding the manor.

"If any bit of the tapestry got left behind, it's most likely in Antoni's house," Erik said, rolling slightly to indicate a nod toward the stone manor.

Brushing past the others, Norah led the way to the manor.

"Who is Antoni?" Greeta said.

"A successful man," Erik said, rolling across the ground next to her. "One hundred years ago invaders stole land belonging to his family. But Antoni's family challenged those invaders and won their land back."

"What happened to him?" The moment Greeta asked the question, she remembered one of the dead men had been called Antoni.

Erik gazed at her steadily and then confirmed her suspicion. "He was standing with my other men inside the ice castle of the dragon goddess before Finehurst destroyed it."

They followed Norah into the stone manor, its doors unlocked. They wandered through a series of spacious rooms, and their footsteps echoed throughout the building. Sunlight streamed through windows streaked with grime, illuminating a constant and thick cloud of dust. Crumbling fireplaces stood empty and dark while a bone-cutting chill filled the air. Although well appointed with furniture, the manor's atmosphere felt empty and haunted by remnants of better days.

Finally, Norah stopped in a large hall, its walls lined with tapestries, illustrated scenes from legends or family history. However, one empty space stood among them.

"There!" Norah cried, running toward the empty space.

The others followed, catching up when she stopped in front of that space. A single strip pooled on the floor beneath that space. Norah hurried to spread it out flat.

Circling it, Greeta stopped and pointed. "This looks like the left side of the tapestry. The pieces we've already put together are the right side and the bottom." Looking closer, Greeta said, "That's where we came from!" She pointed at the image of a small island with a golden spire off the coast of the Northlands. "That's the tower!"

Erik rolled along the side of the tapestry remnant. "The part we're missing shows things like battles and landmarks and maps of all the Upper Lands: the Northlands and Midlands."

"Other!" Norah said, pointing at Njall, who carried the rolled-up partial tapestry made of the other pieces Finehurst had used to bind and control Norah.

Njall rolled it out on the floor while Greeta and Frayka rotated the newly-discovered piece until they discovered how it fit. Once aligned, threads came loose, found each other, and the tapestry pieces wove themselves together.

"Now what?" Njall said.

Norah looked up at them but said nothing.

Remembering her commitment to help

Norah, Greeta said, "We should go back to Tower Island. Even if Finehurst is dead, we might find his sunken ship. What if the rest of the tapestry is on that ship?"

Nodding her approval, Norah led the way back to the wooden Northlander ship.

CHAPTER 37

Retracing their journey, the ship sailed along the rivers of the Southlands to the Midlands and then to the Northlands until the final river met with the sea. Njall and Frayka worked together to adjust the sail to better capture the ocean wind.

Sailing back into the sea, they eventually reached the place where Tower Island had sunk.

The sea bubbled loudly beneath them.

Finehurst's ship of ice flew into the air like a cork held under water too long. Its sides sparkled in the sunlight before it landed upright in the ocean. Once more, seaweed covered the ship.

"There he is," Greeta uttered. "Finehurst

is alive!"

Finehurst stood on the deck of his ice ship, letting his hands rest on the rail. His body seemed to shimmer like a reflection in a quiet lake. He raised his hands and cast them toward the wooden Northlander ship as if hurling an invisible weapon.

The seaweed detached from Finehurst's ice ship and whipped toward the North-landers.

"Uncle Taddeo!" Norah called out.

Stinking of the ocean, giant strips of seaweed landed like heavy tarps on top of the Northlander ship. The force knocked everyone to the deck floor.

Greeta gasped while more strips landed all around her, blocking out light and air. With every piece of seaweed that rained down, she felt the ship gain weight and drop closer to the surface of the water.

The planks of the deck shuddered beneath her.

A wave crashing with white foam caught the Northlander ship and sent it tumbling end over end. The blanket of seaweed caught Greeta and managed to keep her from falling overboard. But when the ship found itself upright, the wave stripped the seaweed away.

Now on her hands and knees on the deck, Greeta flinched at the sudden sunlight and air now washing over the ship. When her eyes adjusted to the light, she saw the mist dragon towering between the Northlander's ship and Finehurst's ship of ice.

"Return what doesn't belong to you!" the mist dragon commanded of Finehurst.

Instead of obeying, Finehurst merely grinned before a sudden breeze sent his ship westward.

Norah called out, "Follow!"

Greeta stood alongside her at the rail, and Erik struggled to keep from rolling across deck with every pitch of the sea. "Something is wrong," Greeta said. "We saw his ship sink here. How can he still be alive?"

"Follow!" Norah said, pointing west. "Now!"

"*Something is wrong*," Greeta insisted. "Why did he lead us to Tower Island? And why would he wait for us to return? What if it's a trap?"

"Finehurst now." Norah remained resolute. "All water dragons, help us!"

The sea surrounding them became calm until the ship might as well have been resting on top of a massive sheet of glass.

Norah leaned far over the railing and touched the still water below. "Uncle," she said, "help me. Ask others to help me." She stood and pointed at Finehurst's ship, speeding west.

The wind whipped the Northlander ship's large square sail and sped the vessel across the flat water.

Greeta clung to the rail more from surprise than the need to steady herself. The ship's speed whipped her hair away from her face, pressing so hard against the air that she struggled for breath. Water sprayed in high arcs on either side of the ship as it parted the sea.

Looking back, Greeta saw Frayka and Njall clinging to the rail on the opposite side of the ship, each struggling to hold on.

The ship sped across the flattened sea for days and nights, but Finehurst's ship remained far ahead despite all efforts to catch up.

Greeta lowered herself to rest on the deck floor, but she felt too much distress to sleep. Frayka had once commented that dragon gods were unpredictable, and Greeta worried about surviving the speed now forced upon the ship by those gods. By morning she rose to her feet, overjoyed to see the familiar coast of the Great Turtle Lands. Although she saw no sign of the beaches near her village, she understood the terrain of her region and recognized it easily. Her village should be no more than a day's journey from here.

Finehurst's ship of ice skimmed along the coastline.

The wooden Northlander ship came to a stop, and the sea began to move with waves again.

Frayka and Njall ran across the deck to join Greeta's side.

"I don't understand," Frayka said. "Where are we?"

"My homeland," Greeta said.

Finehurst's ship of ice changed course and headed south, still skimming the coastline.

A cry from Norah interrupted them. "Uncle!" She held the partial tapestry up toward the sky. Sea spray in the shape of a dragon arose from the ocean, seeming to study the tapestry. A few moments later, the spray exploded, raining down on the deck.

The wooden Northlander ship spun in a new direction to follow Finehurst's ship, knocking Greeta, Frayka, and Njall off their feet. Erik's voice echoed as the ship's momentum forced him to roll across and then below deck.

In the distance, Finehurst's ship of ice paused. Its sail of mist gleamed in the sunlight. Although transparent, it took on the colors and images of a tapestry. Sunbeams travelled through the misty images, and they seemed to come alive. Dragons and men fought until beams of light carried them into the skies above Finehurst's ship. Then those images rushed toward the Northlander ship.

"Uncle!" Norah cried in frustration. "Protect us!"

The clear sky above darkened with clouds rolling in from all directions at once. The sea now churned, pitching the Northlander ship until Njall and Frayka found their way back to the mast and adjusted the sail so that the ship could glide between the violent waves.

Shocked by the storm, Greeta also noticed that it drove away the threatening images sent from Finehurst's ship, which continued to sail ahead of them toward the southern region of the Great Turtle Lands.

The protecting storm surrounded the Northlander ship for hours. Driving rain pelted the deck and drenched them all to the bone. Sickened by the violence of the ship's forward motion, Greeta once again curled up on the deck by the rail, hoping it would end and yet fearing what might happen once it did. The storm persisted until it finally hurled the Northlander ship through the air. The wooden ship landed with a jolt so strong that Greeta found herself ejected from the deck. Moments later she found herself on a white sand beach, wide and stretching along the coast for as far as the eye could see.

Sheets of rain formed a curtain between the sea and sand, making it impossible for Greeta to find the Northlander ship. Sunlight drenched the beach, making it a dry and warm oasis in the middle of the storm.

Did Njall's ship crash apart? What if I'm

RESA NELSON

the only one left alive? What if the others are dead?

The ship of ice slipped through the curtain of rain and glided to a stop on the white sand. The last ice dragon howled, still entrapped as the ship's masthead.

Startled by how close it had landed, Greeta took a step back and tripped. Regaining her balance, she glanced down to see that a polished brown stone the size of a fist had caught her foot.

The ice ship shook itself like a wet dog, shedding drops of water from every surface. The sail made of mist billowed gently.

Squinting, Greeta thought she saw Finehurst standing behind the mist sail. With no one else in sight, Greeta realized she would have to face him alone.

Now is the time to turn into a dragon. But I need to see and feel the signals. I need to feel the ground tremble beneath me. I need to feel my skin itch so I can burst through it.

Greeta concentrated but nothing changed. She closed her eyes with the intent to increase her focus.

I must taste things in the wind. I want to inhale Finehurst's frustration and laugh at its rancid flavor. I need to feel my finger-nails grow into talons.

Her thoughts stirred a fire in her belly. Greeta felt her bones and teeth ache.

But then Finehurst turned sideways to step through the misty sail, and he looked as thin as a sheet of ice. Once he stepped through the sail, he turned to face Greeta.

Finehurst appeared to be no more than a reflection in a mirror. But Finehurst himself wasn't there. Only his reflection on the sheet of ice.

Forgetting her desire to turn into a dragon, Greeta said out loud, "That's why you always looked so strange." Glancing down, she stooped down to pick up the polished stone over which she'd tripped moments ago.

The reflection of Finehurst watched her and smiled.

Greeta took small and slow steps toward him. "I always wondered why someone who likes to talk so much stayed quiet every time we met him."

Finehurst's image shrugged as if Greeta's observation made no difference.

"Why were you at the castle in the Land of Ice?" Greeta felt the heft of the polished stone in the palm of her hand. "Were you a guard left to keep Norah in her place?"

Finehurst's image made a surprised face as if to indicate his secret had been revealed. But then he laughed it off without making a sound.

"Why did you make a ship and leave the castle? Why did you take Njall and leave the Northlander ship behind for us? Why did you lead us to Tower Island in the Northlands and then here to the Great Turtle Lands?"

Finehurst's image shrugged as if he didn't know. Then he laughed soundlessly again.

We took the tapestry pieces from the ice castle. At Tower Island we decided to check the Southlander's home and found another piece there. Now all we need is to take the rest of the tapestry from Finehurst so he can't use it against the gods or any other mortals.

But all Finehurst needs is to take away all the pieces we've gathered. Is that why he led us here? To isolate us in a place where he can steal from us with ease?

The reflection of Finehurst in the sheet of ice shimmered, and steam began to rise from the ship. Fog rolled toward Greeta, threatening to envelope her.

Crying out in anger, Greeta threw the stone at the sheet of ice and shattered it.

Finehurst's image screamed, broke into pieces, and flew into the air. The ship cracked but held together.

Finding another stone on the beach, Greeta ran forward as each fragment of the ice sheet fell on the sand. Each fragment contained a part of Finehurst's reflection, but Greeta used the stone to pound each one.

The screaming stopped, but black smoke curled from each shattered piece of ice and filled in the cracks on the ice ship. The ship, now melting, lifted up into the air and sailed beyond the beach and into the land behind it, vanishing from sight.

Staring at it in dismay, Greeta realized she hadn't paused to think about the consequences of her actions before taking them. She had failed to consider the seven generations.

Have I unwittingly done something good?

Or something bad?

The storm dissipated as quickly as it

had begun. The sheets of rain ended. Dark clouds rolled away, replaced by a hazy sky.

Greeta looked up and no longer found herself alone.

CHAPTER 38

Greeta saw the wooden Northlander ship perched atop a sand bar a short distance away. Frayka and Njall helped each other walk out of the sea and onto shore. Greeta went to meet them.

"Are we still in your homeland?" Frayka said, allowing Njall to cling to her for support.

Greeta scanned the landscape surrounding her. Only the white sands looked familiar. Greeta stared in wonder at the trees where the beach ended, each towering trunk bearing nothing but gigantic fronds at its very top. So unlike the trees surrounding her home, which would all be leafless by now in anticipation of the coming winter. Standing ankle-deep in the water, Greeta noticed its warm temperature, so unlike how frigid the ocean would be near home right now. She also noticed a channel of water running from the edge of the beach into the ocean. And the air itself not only felt warm but far more humid than anything she'd ever experienced before.

Answering Frayka's question, Greeta said, "I think we are still in the Great Turtle Lands, but this looks like a place I've only heard about in legends."

"Legends?" Frayka said, her face crinkling with surprise. "What legends?"

Greeta said, "I think we are near the Land of Swamp Dragons."

Njall took a step back into the water. "If we all work together, we can get our ship free from the sandbar where it landed. We can sail back home."

A loud rumble filled the air. However, the sky had become cloudless, and the rumble seemed to emerge from the sea itself.

Greeta took a deep breath. The months she had spent helping others now made her feel such weariness that dragging one foot in front of the other took all her strength.

But she had promised Papa and Auntie Peppa to help the Northlanders. While in the Dreamtime, she'd promised her mother to help the dragon goddess Norah. "I made a promise to help Norah, and I will keep that promise. No one is safe while Finehurst owns the tapestry with the power to control the gods. I will stay. You can go home."

Greeta remembered something her mother had said.

Whatever it is that binds you also has the power to set you free.

Now Greeta understood her mother's message. The dragon goddess Norah had used a tapestry strip to bind and control Greeta. But once they found Finehurst and recovered the remainder of the tapestry to return to Norah, they would all be free. Finehurst would never be able to control the gods again, much less any mortals.

But a new understanding struck Greeta. Ever since the day Thorkel and Rognvald had taken her away from home, she had resented it and felt burdened. Greeta had spent all that time longing to return to her Shining Star home in the Great Turtle Lands. To return to the family and friends who loved her. To see Red Feather and his brothers who had helped her. All she had wanted was to go back to her normal life and live in peace and quiet.

If I hadn't followed Frayka when the ice dragons came, I would have been on the other side of the chasm with everyone else. Maybe Papa and I would have finished making weapons and then gone home with Auntie Peppa. We'd be in our village now.

But even if Frayka had met Erik and travelled with his men, Norah would have trapped her and Frayka had no means to escape. Norah couldn't have crossed the moat without us. They all would have been trapped when Finehurst destroyed the ice castle. They might have all been killed.

And none of us would know or understand the power that Finehurst has or how to stop him.

My longing to go home was binding me, and choosing to help others and keep my promises to them may be the thing that sets us free from Finehurst.

An incoming wave swept past Greeta's

feet and deposited Erik's head on the beach. Shaking the water off, Erik looked up at her. "If you stay, I stay. Finehurst killed my men and then destroyed them forever. I'll help you find him and get that tapestry back."

Greeta nodded her appreciation. "I don't trust everything we've seen."

"You mean Finehurst and his peculiar ship that he fashioned out of the ice castle?" Frayka said.

Greeta nodded. "I saw Finehurst on his ship just now. But it was some kind of magic image of him. He wasn't real. Since we first saw him at the ice castle, he always looked and acted peculiar." She decided to wait to tell them about destroying the image only to watch it turn into smoke.

"Real or not," Erik said, "We chased Finehurst down. We need to find out if he survived before it costs us our lives."

"Best of luck to you all." Njall took a few steps into the sea toward the ship. "Let's go, Frayka. We have just enough time to get home before winter locks us out."

Frayka stood her ground, withdrawing the knife still tucked under her belt. She shook beads of water from the blade. "We'll need to find whetstones for grinding away rust and sharpening edges." Glancing at Greeta, she said, "You still have your sword?"

Greeta clamped her hand on the scabbard by her side, feeling the blade within. "I do."

Frayka called out to Njall. "Tell our people we're fine."

Sighing heavily, Njall stood in the water and looked from Frayka to the wooden Northlander ship and back at Frayka again. Moments later, he splashed his way back onto the beach. "And have them ridicule me for being a coward?" When everyone stared at him, Njall said, "Where you go, I go."

His words felt like the warming rays of the sun. Greeta remembered what her mother had told her.

People are like swords. You don't know whether their character is weak or strong until they're tested by strife.

Greeta realized everyone surrounding her had been tested relentlessly. Frayka and Njall had proven themselves to be brave warriors, willing to fight at a moment's notice. Although Erik had lost all his companions, he had helped at every step. They all wanted different things: Frayka needed Njall to father children who would inherit her gift for portents, Njall had come in search of Frayka and Greeta to take them back to Blackstone, and Erik sought revenge against Finehurst. And yet they had all worked together when it counted. They had proven themselves to be trustworthy and reliable. And perhaps even caring.

A strange feeling overwhelmed Greeta. Although she still missed Papa, Auntie Peppa, and the Shining Star people, being with Frayka and Njall and Erik felt like home. She no longer felt burdened.

Despite the difficulties they'd most likely soon be facing, Greeta felt light. Home no longer felt like sleeping in a familiar bed or eating familiar food or seeing the faces of people she'd known all her life.

Home now felt like the welcome company of three Northlanders, two living and one dead, who shared Greeta's vision of what mattered.

Greeta said, "When the tide comes in, we can sail the ship over the sandbar and onto the beach. The ship can be our shelter. We should look for whetstones and food and kindling to make a fire." Pointing at the narrow channel of water bisecting the beach that she'd noticed moments ago, Greeta said, "I imagine that water is trickling down from a stream nearby. Fresh water."

Njall reached down to pick up Erik, rescuing him from an incoming wave that might have swept him back out to sea. Tucking Erik's head under his arm, Njall said, "You're saying we'll be safe?"

Greeta met his gaze. "I'm saying we need to be prepared before we begin our search for Finehurst."

When her friends nodded their agreement, Greeta felt happy to be home.

ABOUT THE AUTHOR

When Resa Nelson's short story "The Dragonslayer's Sword" was first published in *Science Fiction Age* magazine, it ranked 2nd in that magazine's first Readers Top Ten poll. Around the same time, the manager of a major bookstore contacted the magazine editor asking how to buy the novel because many of his customers were asking to buy it.

No such novel existed. Only the short story existed. Readers assumed it had come from a novel.

This is when Resa realized all her readers are smarter than she is, because they knew there was more to the story. It only took her eight years to figure out what they already knew. She plans to write at least four series that take place in her Dragonslayer World. Series #1 (Dragonslayer Series) is complete. *Dragonfly* is Book 1 in the Dragonfly series.

Visit Resa's website at
www.resanelson.com and follow her on
Twitter at @ResaNelson.

Made in the USA
Las Vegas, NV
03 February 2023

66729498R00190